Pay It Backward
Faith In Action Series Book 2

Megy Davis

Megan Davis

Pay It Backward by Megy Davis

Copyright © 2023, 2019, 2012 by Megy Davis

Identifiers: Library of Congress Control Number: 2023912179

eBook ISBN: 9781618428356

Paperback ISBN: 9781733141734

Scripture taken from THE MESSAGE. Copyright © 1993, 1994, 1995, 1996, 2000, 2001, 2002. Used by permission of NavPress Publishing Group.

Used by permission of Zondervan Bible Publishers. (See Bibliography for Bible quotes)

Published in the United States of America by Megan Davis

Cover design by Mars Dorian

Created with Atticus

Visit my store at: https://www.megydavis.com/

Email me at: megydavis@megydavis.com

Insta: megydavis_author_photographer

Threads: @megydavis_author_photographer@threads.net

https://www.Facebook.com/SaltOfLifeFiction

Contents

1

New Times

I jump to my feet on the top row of the bleachers, whistling, cheering, and high fiving with the other members of the Addison family. My new family. My new high school. This is incredible. Jose and I have gone from being homeless runaways to living with a loving, caring family.

There goes Jose, racing over and handing Sara a towel as she pulls herself out of the pool after an amazing high dive. Ha ha! Now he's all wet, too. It didn't take Jose long to fall in love with our new sister. Or sorta sister. For now. And our sorta brother, Luke. This adoption business is tricky. We'll see. It's only been a month.

For now, they say I can swim for the Boca South Swim Team with Luke and Sara. I don't know. That chlorine smell could be a real deal breaker. Burns my eyes. Now that we're safe, I want to wait a bit. Check out different ways to spend my free time. Free time. I didn't miss it until I didn't have it, working seven days a week at the circus. Like before Mommy and Poppy were killed. Church, school, art class. This way of life is unreal most days. Yet here I am. I wipe the sweat from my forehead.

"It takes forever for the dive team score to post." Mrs. Addison leans in and pats my arm as we sit. I freeze for a quick second. While her momentary touch is comforting, it's still unfamiliar. It startles me when she does it, and she does it often. She is one of those touchy-feely moms. Mommy was too. I like it, but how can I be sure Mrs. Addison will always be there for us?

"Help yourself to a cold drink from the cooler. Don't be shy, Pedro. Jose isn't." Jose has the cooler open and is pawing through the ice, looking for a drink.

That must be the opposing team's parent section across the pool, under the scoreboard. It's tough to see past the glare of the afternoon sun on the pool water. I pull my new sunglasses down for a better look. Sara said we were competing against a team from Miami. Boca Raton is as far south as I ever want to live again. If I never return to Miami, it will be fine with me.

That guy looks familiar. Whaa— Can't be? Here? No way! I stand up, my body tensing. My heart is pounding, sweat forming on the back of my neck. What are the chances that a loser like him would be at this swim meet? At this pool? In this city? Killers don't go to high school swim meets. Wait! Would I even remember him after so many months?

Whoa! If it is him, he might recognize me. He did glare at me through the window that day—the day he killed Mommy and Poppy. Stared straight into my eyes for a full second. I'll never forget those eyes. Like snake eyes. Hands shaking, I shove my sunglasses back down over my eyes and pull my cap down. I sink down onto the bleachers, my knees weak. Mrs. Addison glances over at me. A half smile ... all I can muster.

If he sees me today, Jose and I will be in danger ... again. On the run ... again. I thought we were finally safe. Would I always have to watch our backs? Heart pounding in my ears, I stare into the rippling pool of water, barely able to breathe. Got to stop this doomsday thinking. That creep doesn't even know I exist. Deep breath.

The score posts, and the man stands, clapping. Short and bald, with a big belly. It is him! Standing up, I take a step backward. My foot slips, and I nearly tumble off the top of the bleachers. I grab the guardrail just in time, meeting Mrs. Addison's startled look. Pull yourself together, dude. Got to go check it out.

"Be right back," I mumble to Mrs. Addison, pulling my hat halfway down my face. I wind my way to the pool deck, never taking my eyes off the man in the crowd. The sound of my flip flops on the metal and my heart thumping inside my chest are the only sounds in my ears.

I'll stand over here, behind the fence. Watch them. Two guys. Super rough looking. Why wear dark slacks, sports jackets, and shiny black dress shoes to a swim meet? Sweaty and out of place, they look as if they're headed to the casino rather than spending a blistering afternoon in the glaring sun.

Yes! The dude on the right is the owner of the crack house in Hialeah!

"Who are those guys?" Luke has walked up behind me and I tense. Relax.

"Street dudes I recognize from when I lived in Hialeah. Hey, Luke, can you take a picture of them with your phone when they're not looking? I left my phone in my backpack."

"Sure. Hold these." Luke gives me a pile of papers. I turn toward him so I won't be seen. Pretending to be texting, Luke zooms in and takes their photo.

Letting out a pent-up breath, I stare at the image on Luke's phone. "Yep. That is absolutely the guy. Thanks, bro. Send it to me, please?" I hand the papers back. The columns of names and numbers don't make sense at first glance. "Hey, what are these?"

"Heat sheets. You buy them at the entrance. Two bucks. They detail who's swimming, where and when, by the swim stroke, school, and the athlete's name. See?" Luke points to his name in the maze of data. "The next time I swim is in five minutes, at 3:00, lane five, butterfly. Gotta go."

"Good luck, bro. Swim fast." I need my own heat sheet to track the swimmer those guys are watching. Maybe then I can get a name.

As I walk over to the entrance, a roar rises from the Boca South section. The scoreboard posts a 9.3 for Sara's dive. I need to be over there whooping it up with the family. This is my life now. Biting my lip, I try to rewind to ten minutes ago. To when I was living the dream. Safe, secure, adopted. Jose needs the dream. I need the dream.

Nope. If that guy is walking free, this new life, this safe life, is now on pause. I need to watch these two guys to see who they cheer for when the Miami team, Callahan, swims. Is one of them a swim dad? Who else but a parent would come out in this sweltering heat to watch a student swim for a few seconds?

The blare of the horn pierces the air. Six swimmers enter the water. There! They stand to cheer for the swimmer in lane three. Or was it lane four? The heat sheet shakes as my trembling finger finds first the stroke, the school, and then the swimmer's name. Callahan High in three and a Boca swimmer in four. I let out a long breath. Lane three. Okay. I have a name. Justin Espinoza. That's a start. This makes my job easy. Jose, trust me, this running from Mommy and Poppy's killer is going to end once and for all.

Stepping behind a pole, I sag against it. Sweat drips off my face and neck. Pulling my Boca South t-shirt off, I mop my face, neck, and forehead. When my heartrate returns to normal, I run my fingers through my hair, tucking it tight behind my ears. Taking a deep breath, I put my hat and sunglasses on and walk toward the bleachers. My adoptive family.

This is not good. I've been gone for too long. Mrs. Addison is glancing my way again. Please don't ask questions. She's chill. Never too nosy about my past. I sure can't explain it to her today. Cramming the heat sheets into my back pocket, I put a smile on my face and start up the steps.

Looking back, I notice the two dudes have disappeared. I look up at the scoreboard. Justin Espinoza has won the heat. Why didn't that guy, if it is his dad, stick around to see his son claim his victory? Under my breath, I repeat the name Espinoza over and over. Each time I do, my jaw gets tighter and tighter. We will meet face-to-face, Espinoza. Count on it. In my gut, I know what you did.

How can I explain to my new mom that her adoptive son has just seen his parents' murderer? How could she ever understand that I've been planning a painful revenge every single night for the past year and a half? Cracking my neck and shrugging, I move across the bench to sit next to Jose. I give him a fierce hug. Once again, I'm outside the dream, looking in.

Late that night, I lie wide awake, fists clenched, mesmerized by the shadows of the palm tree outside my window sweeping across the ceiling. Jose sleeps next to me, snoring every so often. Like so many nights before, I methodically and violently fantasize about my revenge on the man who stole our parents from us. How he'd suffer, as my brother and I have suffered, homeless and at the mercy of a brutal circus owner. Mounting waves of black rage wash over me as I consider various revenge scenarios. Now I have a face. A name.

I haven't had these thoughts in the past month, since the circus train explosion changed our lives for the better. Today, seeing the man from that Hialeah crack house brought those painful memories and images back, more vivid than ever.

Sliding off the bed, I sit on the floor. My back against the mattress with eyes closed, I roll my head back and forth ... calming myself ... trying to defuse my rage.

Not working. I get up and pace. When I felt this way while working at the Festival Circus, I'd find Big Dee's bottle of rum and drink myself to sleep. Do the Addisons keep liquor in the house? As quietly as I can, I creep downstairs and search the cabinets in the TV room, patio, and kitchen. Nothing. I settle for Sara's cookies.

Should I try to pray? True, I asked Jesus Christ into my heart, but is that really the answer to this black hole in my soul? It seems to work for the rest of the family. Focus on forgiveness? Not tonight. Even if I wanted to pray, where would I begin? I need rum, and I need it now. Somehow, I'll get a bottle.

Back in bed, I look at Jose's peaceful, sleeping face. His happiness is my number one priority. I need to do whatever it takes to ensure that. I owe that to Mommy and Poppy. Staring at the never-ending motion of the shadow of that palm tree on my ceiling, I wait for sleep to come.

2

Great Day

"That's it?" I look up at Doc Wainwright from the exam table in his office. He just finished removing the four polydactylies from my hands and feet. The procedure took less than an hour. Lifelong embarrassing pieces of flesh, now replaced by four small bandages. Never stressing again when meeting new people. Taking a deep breath, I smile at Doc.

Hopping off the table as if I'm weightless, I laugh, bringing my hands up in front of my face, amazed. There are no words for this moment—the moment I wished for, hoped for, had finally given up on. Today, through the goodness of one man, it's done! I hug him. Hard. Hugs aren't my thing, but I can't help myself.

"That's it!" Doc booms when I finally let go. "Don't get your hands or feet wet for five days. Clean them frequently with towelettes and you'll be as good as new this time next week. Just in time for our first UM football game of the season. All you kids are invited. Dana and I have a skybox. Haven't missed an opening game since 1987!" This man, with his loud voice and generosity, is larger than life. How do I respond to such kindness? I nod my head and continue to look from my hands to my feet. Mommy and Poppy had been saving for this operation for years, but something always came up. And then they were killed.

"Thank you, sir. I wish my parents were here to see this. This was their great wish for me."

"Delighted to do it, kid! Times like this make being a doctor the best line of work imaginable. Now go on. Get out of here. Be a teenager. See you on game day. We'll do a follow-up exam there." He laughs, walking me out to the front office, where Mrs. Addison is waiting.

Friday afternoon and everyone is away, doing their own thing. No problem being home alone. I like it. Last week, Mrs. Addison walked up to me working crossword puzzles on the back page of the newspaper. The next day I found a puzzle book and dictionary at my breakfast spot. My throat had squeezed shut. I couldn't speak. What a thoughtful thing to do! I gave her my first mom hug in a very long time. Now I call out to anyone who will answer to help me discover or spell a word.

The cuckoo clock strikes 1:00. Smiling, I think back to the look on Mrs. Addison's face when she came home from food shopping. I had their family's antique cuckoo clock lying in hundreds of tiny parts on the kitchen table. The clock didn't work, but they kept it on the wall because it was a cool piece of carved Austrian wood. It had been in their family since World War ll. Before she finished cooking dinner, I had the clock assembled and working perfectly. Now we celebrate at the top of every hour because a hand-painted cuckoo bird comes out and does a dance to a tune named "Edelweiss." Nobody had seen that bird for seventy-five years.

If possible, I never miss a forensics-based cop show on TV. Mr. Addison and I have two favorites that we watch every night after dessert. Of the four of us, I seem to enjoy hanging around the house the most. Every day is like a holiday, with family coming and going, talking about their day.

As my gut reacts to random stuff, I know I'm still unwinding from the events of our recent past. I don't have the need to go out and do stuff—or just hang out. I've needed a place to call home since they hauled us away from our townhome in Hialeah in the middle of the night. I already know what's happening out there in the streets. I've lived there. Survived there. Homeless.

Yep, staying in is fine with me. I've run into enough strange people and weird situations to last a lifetime. Maybe that's a negative way of thinking. I may get over it. Maybe not. Who knows? For now, I'm happy to have the company of a "mom" to bounce ideas off. Someone to be there for me when I have to sort out problems, someone to help me define my "new normal." Especially after a year of hiding. Living on the run from the police. In perpetual fear of Big Dee and his bullwhip.

Flipping on the computer, I stare at my bandaged baby fingers. Wow! Keyboarding is so much smoother. Thank you, Doc! Thank you a hundred times. And thank you, Luke, for setting me up with an email address and showing me how to google info. Sara even set up a couple of social media accounts for me. Not that I know anybody other than the Addisons and Danny.

What about Justin Espinoza? Opening my social media feed, I type in his name and scroll through lots of hits. That's a popular Latino name. Studying the hometown stats, I find a Justin in Hialeah and click on him. Justin's interests are surfing, swimming, and Modern Warfare. Modern Warfare? What's that? I google it. It's an internet gaming site. I check it out. Kill or get killed seems to be the object of the game. The Addisons don't have the gaming device I need to play, but there seem to be tons of other hunt and kill games on the net.

Wow! Hunting and killing bad guys is a blast. This is so real, with machine gun sounds and actual human noises of pain and death. No learning curve needed. Vengeance is mine. It's so easy to get lost in the action.

I hear the crunch of gravel and glance out the window. Danny's car is turning into the driveway. What time is it? The wall clock reads 4:00 PM. I've been gaming for three hours. Checking my score, I log off. Not bad for a first timer. Do the Addisons approve of computer gaming? Probably not.

"Hey, hey! Where's the patient?" Danny, Luke, and Sara swarm around me to check out my hands and feet. Sticking out my arms and legs, I grin.

"Gone! How cool is that, Pedro?" Danny takes my hands, examining my bandages.

"Yeah, even now I barely remember how they looked. This is a new starting point for me. Nobody at Boca South has seen those awful things. I'll never have to feel odd or explain what they are again."

"Does it hurt?" Danny asks. I shake my head.

"It's a great day," Sara exclaims. "How shall we celebrate?"

"Pedro needs to keep his cuts dry. So, we can't go to the beach," Luke says.

"I have practice at church with the praise band at 7:00," Sara says. "You guys could hang out and watch. In the meantime, I can throw a pizza together for supper. Mom, Dad, and Jose should be home shortly."

"Sounds like a plan. I'm hungry." Danny invites himself over for dinner—as usual. "Would you sing the song you sang the day we captured Big Dee? That seems like a million years ago."

"'*He is Here*?' Sure Danny. I'm happy you like it." Sara heads for the kitchen, and Danny follows her.

3

Hope

Saturday comes and I wake up late. Half asleep, I roll over and feel Jose's empty spot. He's gone! My stomach tightens. Opening my eyes, I realize where I was. Jose and I are safe with the Addisons.

Yes, Jose and Mrs. Addison are going to the library this morning. Jose felt odd, being the oldest kid in his seventh-grade class. Mrs. Addison decided to tutor him through both seventh and eighth grades this year. Jose said he was up for the challenge. The tough part is that he reads slowly, with his lazy eye and patch. It's awesome to watch a special bond forming between them.

I draw in a deep breath and grin, my heart seeming to grow inside my chest. "Thank you, Jesus." A brief prayer. That's all I can get out these days. I quit praying the day they killed Mommy and Poppy. True, I'm living with a seriously praying family. Way down deep I don't have the faith and trust they take for granted. "Why did You neglect us for so long? Why, God?"

As I watch Luke pull every cereal box we have from the cupboard and put them on the counter, I pour myself a cup of coffee. Silently, Sara brings out the bowls, spoons, and milk. After pouring herself a bowl of Chocolate Lucky Stars, she sits, continuing to read the box, front and back. Danny plops himself next to Sara.

He goes through the boxes, reading the titles out loud. "Krunchy Krispys, Funny Flakes, Nine Nuts, Brown Bran…" Sara gives a thumbs up or down. These two are a pair. Picking up the Brown Bran, I turn it over and find nothing of interest. Less than nothing.

"What's the big deal with cereal boxes?" I put it back in the line-up.

"So much information." Sara swallows her Lucky Stars. "Here on the bottom and side is all the nutritional info. On the back is a recipe using the cereal—and a picture! Look, I could make that, Chocolate Lucky Stars brownies."

"I always look for the expiration date before I pour myself a bowl." Danny points to the hard-to-read date on the box top.

Luke asks Danny, "Hey, what time are we taking off for the big city today?" We've been planning our trip to Miami all week. This is a big deal, the first University of Miami football game of the season.

"Kickoff is at 8:00. So, five-ish?"

"Works for me," Luke says.

"Is Cheree coming?" Sara looks at Luke.

"Yeah. Her dad said she could take off early from work for the game. His car dealership is taking part in that Cash 4 Clunkers program the government is promoting. She said they've been overrun with car buyers this past week. Even her mom is helping."

"Yeah, I heard about that. You bring in your old car, and the government reimburses the dealer up to $2000 as a down payment," Sara says.

"There's lots and lots of paperwork. That's what Cheree's doing. I'd be happy with one of those clunkers." Luke's dream for a car is on hold. For now. He either has to grab a ride with Danny or catch a ride with Cheree in her brand new Mustang convertible. Not bad choices. They always invite me along.

"Yeah. It should be fun. You, me, Cheree, Danny, and Pedro." Luke swallows the last of his Krunchy Krispies.

Late that afternoon, Danny merges onto I-95 South toward Miami. I kick back for the long ride, ready to unwind and have a good time. I haven't been back to Miami since I left the foster care group home. The bright orange sun fades in and out as we speed past towering downtown skyscrapers. My hometown. A familiar, almost forgotten sight. My stomach flutters, won't settle. Somewhere in this cement jungle, Espinoza is walking free.

The day I left this place seems like a million years ago. Fifteen years old, jumping a train to anywhere. Today I return. With good friends, reliable friends—and a new brother and sister. I miss you, Mommy and Poppy. Squeezing my eyes shut, I will the heartbreak away. For now.

"We're here," Danny sings out as we turn into the Orange Bowl Stadium parking area. A live football game with cheering crowds, people wearing their crazy orange and green clothes, and face paint. I've only seen it on TV. Time to enjoy the moment. Every moment. So easy with these guys.

"You made it!" Doc booms as we walk into the upper deck skybox. Wow! The view of the playing field is fantastic. And this large party place is stocked with enough food and drinks to feed an army. A banquet. Open bottles of rum and whiskey on the bar.

A dull roar begins in my ears, and I can hear myself breathing. Time stops. No way will I touch that bottle. I hate this temptation, this desire that jumped out of nowhere. Doc and Dana are generous people, despite their fame as innovative physicians. Innovative, a crossword puzzle word yesterday. They invited us here to enjoy the game.

Time to concentrate on the good in my life, not the booze or the past. Running my fingers through my hair and tucking it tight behind my ears, I walk over to the group at the long window overlooking the field.

"Pedro! Let me shake your hand!" Doc smiles. Grasping my hand, he gives it a firm shake, then turns it over and examines it. "You're completely healed."

"It doesn't even hurt." I laugh. "I can't thank you enough, Doc."

"Watching you reach out to shake my hand with no hesitation ... that is thank you enough for me, son." Doc smiles. He glances around, then says, "Grab yourself some BBQ and check out the game, or the sunset." He gestures to the west as the fiery orange ball slips into the Everglades.

"Everybody, meet Danny's older brother, Andy," Dana says as Andy comes into the skybox. Proud mom. I can tell by the way she looks at Andy. Danny gives his brother a long hug. Andy resembles Dana, taller than Danny, with light brown hair and the same color eyes. Andy shakes our hands all around. He seems more serious, more reserved than Danny. Dana declares, putting her arm around Andy's waist, "Miami criminals, beware! My son, the future forensic scientist, will clean up the streets when he graduates in May!"

"Never get in a room alone with my dad," Luke says. "He'll talk your ear off about the cold cases he watches on TV."

"Yeah, Pedro here, too." Danny looks at me. "He loves that stuff." I shake Andy's hand. Yes, I will corner Andy about March 2022. These burning questions about my parents' death are driving me nuts. Maybe Andy knows where to look for answers. Any way around it, I'm not leaving here tonight without speaking to him in private.

The opportunity happens sooner than I expect. At halftime, the Wainwrights, Sara, Luke, and Cheree walk over to the skybox next door. Andy stays behind, manning the grill. I stick around to help him.

"Danny told me about the situation with you and your brother, Pedro. Sounds like a wild ride, especially for kids your age." Andy looks up from the hot dogs he's turning. Ugh, the smell of hot dogs! I back away a few feet.

"Yeah, you could say that. We used to live in Hialeah, west of the Palmetto Expressway. Do you know where Ave Maria Cemetery is?"

"Yeah. It's a lot farther south than Hialeah. Out in West Kendall. Is that where your folks are buried?"

"That's what we were told. I've never been there. So, I don't know. Everything happened so quickly when my parents were killed. They took Jose and I away that same night to a care facility for kids. Hey, Andy, can you explain to me how to find information about my parents' accident?" I glance at the door, tensing at the thought that someone might come in before I get info from Andy. Any info.

"Sure. What's on your mind?" Yes! Here's the invitation I was hoping for. As Andy and I talk, I feel I can trust him. I pour out the full story as rapidly as possible. As I speak, his face grows serious. He sinks down in a chair, listens without interrupting. He motions for me to sit with him, shaking his head, frowning as if not believing my story. I have his complete attention. When I finish, Andy puts his elbows on the table, clasps his hands together, tapping them over his mouth. Saying nothing for a long moment. I squirm. Does he believe me? Who would make this stuff up?

"I don't know of any police department that operates that way, Pedro. Let's go over your story again. Slower this time." Quietly, Andy asks questions, shaking his head and sometimes narrowing his eyes at my answers.

The rest of the group straggles in for the second half. Andy asks, "Are you guys coming to the game next Saturday?" I nod. "Okay, bring everything you have of your parents'. Photos, jewelry, anything. In the meantime, I'll talk to my professor. He may let me reopen their cold case as my master's project. It's interesting and a major challenge. I'll start digging around on my end."

"Wow! That's more than I would ever expect or ask. Thanks, Andy. Message me if you need anything else, okay?"

"Perfect. This helps me, too, because I require a master's project to graduate. What's your number?" Taking out his phone, he calls me. Connected. Just like that!

Now I can enjoy the rest of the game. Touchdown! Jumping up, I pump my fists, yelling and cheering with the rest. With a meaningful look, Doc high fives me. Together, we shout the school song displayed on the big screens and make a toast for every yard gained. It's exhausting having so much fun!

I'm fine if I hang with everybody else in front of the skybox and keep my eyes on the field, but the fully stocked bar taunts me. Left alone, I fish a can of cola out of the cooler and pour half of it out. Making sure the corridor is empty, I duck back inside and top off my can with rum. Returning the bottle to the bar, I twirl the liquid in the can. Wow! This is too easy.

Taking a long drink, I hold my breath, waiting for the relaxing effect to take hold. Half-empty can in hand, I wander over to the grill. I put the last plump hot dog into my mouth. Look at me now, Big Dee. Drinking rum and eating gourmet tube steaks. Today I'm in a deluxe skybox overlooking the city of Miami while you rot in jail. Next up: Craig Espinoza.

The ride home is how a great day should end. In the back seat, Luke and Cheree are curled up next to me, with Danny and Sara in the front. My entire being is relaxed, a smile pasted on my face—put there by the alcohol. Feeling great. It has been a long while. Clearly it's the rum. I'm at peace with my mission. Andy sounds all in, too.

Until I put the man who murdered Mommy and Poppy behind bars, this is how it must be. They were murdered in cold blood. I'm positive of it.

My friends and family have fun, oblivious to what is churning inside my mind. Their cares don't include this gnawing need for revenge, dulled only by stolen rum. My need to get on with simple living is powerful, but not as powerful as the deeper desire to know my parents' murderers are in prison. And I will put them there. Only then can I get on with enjoying life to the max.

4

Brotherly Advice

The first full week of school is a blur. I'm the same age as Luke and Sara but a year behind in my classes. Walking through the front doors of Boca High makes it feel like I never left school. Once I get into the flow of my schedule, it will be easy to study for hours, like I used to. Reading and notetaking are my superpowers. And art class! My art teacher seems to like what she does, running around the classroom all inspired, all the things a teacher should be and do. I wonder what we'll be working on first. Oils and acrylics, I hope. Can't wait.

That night, Sara and I study together at a long desk in the den. The sounds of the house fade away as I concentrate on memorizing Academic Spanish. I know Cuban Spanish, but it's not the same as they teach here. The differences in dialect fascinate me. I make notes of every word and verb conjugation I need to learn for the course. Easy and hard at the same time. I'm up for the challenge!

Sara leans back in her chair, putting her feet up on the desk. Her history textbook is open to the title page of the chapter, her notebook blank. She chews on her plastic pen tip, staring out the window. Definitely not into it.

"Earth to Sara." I reach over and nudge her shoulder.

She looks over at me, frustrated. "I despise school, I detest chemistry, and I loathe homework!" Wow! This side of Sara is new to me. I figured her for an honor student. She's so good at so many other things. Guess not. Maybe I can help her.

"I know. But you have to do it. I'll help you with American History if you need it."

"That's sort of interesting. Even though we're studying what happened in the 1700s. But why can't we learn what's going on today?"

"Like what's going on between you and Danny?"

Her eyes brighten, and she grins. "Yeah. Stuff like that. Fun stuff."

"So, what is happening with you and Danny? Traveling with the circus, I saw enough romances to know chemistry when I see it," I tease.

"Yeah?"

"Yeah. You two got it."

"Yeah." She smiles even bigger, looking out the window again. I tap her open book with my pencil. She laughs. "Okay, okay, I'm focusing." A minute later, she looks up at me. "You and Andy were thicker than thieves at the game Saturday. He's a serious dude, completely the opposite of Danny. That was the first time I'd met him."

"We were talking about how my parents were killed and if there was a police case. He sounded disappointed in the police investigation. I was just a kid in shock and don't recall many of the details."

"I'm so sorry, Pedro. So much to deal with..."

"Yeah. I was dazed. And watching out for Jose. Obsessed with watching out for him."

"I love that kid!" Sara says. "He's so outgoing and has a personality you instantly fall in love with."

"Only lately. Two weeks ago, he never smiled and was too scared to talk to anyone but me. He cried a lot at night when he thought I was asleep. That broke my heart even more. You and your family are a gift from heaven. Anyway, Andy told me he'd be interested in investigating our cold case as part of his school project. He needs to complete one case study to graduate. Saturday he wants me to bring the things the foster care people gave me after they took us from our home. He thinks there may be a clue there to follow. I can't wait."

"A win-win. I can't wait for Saturday either. We had a blast at the stadium. Danny wants to show me some of the fun places he explored as a kid. It's an enormous place!"

"Yeah! So, you never answered my question. What is going on with you and Danny?" I turn to her.

Jose comes into the den and echoes, "Yeah! So, what is going on with you and Danny?" Wiggling in between the two of us, he hangs his arms around our necks.

"We're just having fun." Sara grins. "The attraction is so unlikely. But he's been around the block a few times with other girls, if you know what I mean. So, I don't know. I do like the way he always makes me laugh."

"I think he likes you a bunch, Sara. He'd be dumb not to. I have the most beautiful big sister in Boca." We both laugh as Jose runs his fingers through Sara's thick brown hair. "Can I brush it, Sara? I brushed my mom's hair when I was growing up."

"Sure, Jose." She leans over to pull a pick out of her bag. "But use this. A brush will make my hair frizzy." Jose listens as Sara and I continue to talk about Danny.

"He's a solid dude all around," I say. "Just be careful. Go slow. I can see you don't have much experience with guys."

"Don't I know it?" Sara giggles. "Okay, enough of this Danny talk. Let's get to work."

"I'll leave you two to this important high school stuff. I have serious TV watching to do with Mom and Dad." Jose drops Sara's pick back into her bag.

"Thanks, Jose." Sara kisses him on the cheek. "I'll come find you when my ego needs a boost. Or when I need my hair fixed!"

"Jose, did you finish your homework? I know you have a test coming up. You can watch TV anytime." I turn to him.

"I'm ready for my math test. I just can't decide what to do for my semester science project. I remember you did something real cool with batteries. Can you help me come up with two ideas I can hand in to the teacher?" Jose asks.

"That I can, little bro. I'll think about it, and we can brainstorm tomorrow night. Okay?"

"Yep! Gotta go. If you miss the first few minutes of '*Ordinance and Order*,' you miss the clues to solve the case before the cops do. See ya!" Jose bolts from the den.

"Pedro..." Sara smiles. "Jose has Mom, Dad, Luke, and I as a support system, too. Relax. Don't worry about him so much. I know he wants your help but have fun with it. It's not all on your shoulders anymore."

"You're right. Force of habit, I guess. I was his age when Mommy and Poppy were taken from us. I can't get that time back. So, I want to make it as good as I can for him. Sounds stupid, I guess. These days he actually sleeps with a smile on his face."

"It doesn't sound stupid. What about you, Pedro? Do you sleep with a smile on your face?" Sara asks.

"I'm lucky to even fall asleep. I don't sleep much." Running my fingers through my hair, I tuck it tight behind my ears.

5

Personal Treasures

Later, alone in my room, I set out the few items I still have from my childhood. Do I have the strength to do this? It's been a long time. Taking a long breath, I recognize the lead-like feeling settling in my gut. My fingers run over Mommy's things: her wedding ring, the gold cross from her necklace, and the amethyst earring she was wearing the day she passed. Tears sting my eyes.

Touching the envelope of family photos, I close my eyes tight. Nope, not ready for these just now. Laying the packet next to my last report card from Hialeah High, I pick up the children's Bible Mommy and Poppy gave me for my First Holy Communion. I open it to see our parents' death certificates. Also, a yellowing newspaper clipping reporting their deaths as a casualty by an unknown hit and run driver. Five lines of newsprint, nothing more. How can five lines of newsprint be the end of my parents? The period at the end of that last sentence ... the end of their existence.

An unknown hit and run driver? I know who you are, Espinoza. And soon everybody will know. In one swift motion, I grab my backpack and hurl it against the wall, heart hammering inside my chest, blood pounding in my ears.

"Killer!" I yell. Then I freeze. Who heard me? I peer out the bedroom door, down the stairs. No movement. Only the distant sound of canned laughter from the TV in the family room.

And where are Poppy's things? He never laid block with his wedding ring on. But he always put it on when he came home from work, right after showering. Then they went for their nightly walk. Where is his ring? In a gutter somewhere in the streets of Hialeah? Sweeping my fingers over the raised letters of his death certificate finalizes everything. Tears sting the back of my eyes again. Blinking, I will them away.

Sorting through these few items is a huge energy suck. Picking up my bag, I put what is left of my past inside the smallest compartment, zipping it up. Slumping into the chair, I sit motionless, tears dripping from my chin. Lately, that's all I have, tears. Robbed of the heaving sobs that used to bring relief. Bitterness is paralyzing me, again leaving a nasty taste in my mouth. At the very bottom of my bag, I fish out a Cuban Lunch, the piece of candy Mommy put in my school lunch bag that last day. It was always our dessert. She knew they were my favorite. Wiping my tears off the bright yellow and blue cellophane wrapper, I tear it open, smell it, then chew the sweet chocolate.

I know exactly what I'll do when I meet Espinoza. I think of little else ... I never hoped to have someone like Andy lead me straight to him. I'd envisioned coming back to Miami and stalking the crack house until Espinoza came out. I'd follow him, then smash him from behind with a baseball bat, leaving him on the pavement. Yeah, I think through this scenario every now and then until my fury subsides, but the pain never goes away completely.

As a student, Andy probably has strict rules and regulations to follow. He has the University of Miami and the Miami-Dade police force with all its modern technology at his fingertips. For his semester project, he must prove or disprove, without any doubt, whether this Espinoza guy is responsible for manslaughter. How will we manage that? Our case is almost eighteen months old. Are we shooting in the dark? I turn my cell on and stare at the picture of Espinoza for the thousandth time. This is the guy. I don't know who the other guy is. He looks shady, too. His partner?

Sure, this is opposite of what I'm learning as a Christian. But I'd resolved to get my bloody revenge long before I met the Addisons. I can't let go of this fierce need to make Espinoza suffer. I want to. But more than that, I need to see him bleed, need to hear him cry out in pain. Like those guys in the computer kill games. When will this burning hate disappear? This all-consuming passion and hate that steals the joy from my new life. My deal with Andy is the only thing holding me back from carrying out this crazy impulse to do something extreme tonight.

Where's the rum when I need it? I grab my backpack and dig around the bottom for a smoke. Big Dee used to give me cigarettes on the days he was feeling especially generous. Late at night, I'd roam around the circus trailers and tents, enjoying a cigarette before bedding down on the hard ground in my sleeping bag. I liked the solitude and cool night air. Even sleeping under the stars. My fingers touch a single cigarette. I pull it out. It's slightly mangled, but it will do. I take my lighter from the side pocket.

"I'm going for a walk," I call to Mr. Addison as I open the front door. He knows I enjoy being outside at night and is okay with it. Most nights I sit on the front porch steps. Tonight is different. Still reeling inside, I need to chill out.

Stopping halfway up the driveway, I light my cigarette, inhaling deep. A few more pulls and I come close to feeling normal. Why are my old habits becoming necessary for my sanity and spilling over into this life? I walk to the stop sign at the end of the street, inhaling the last of my cigarette, my last cigarette. A part of me deflating with every exhale. That familiar heavy feeling settling over me again. A sadness I can't share. Who would understand? Who could?

6

Miami Game Day

Saturday, Andy and I sit huddled at a back table in the skybox, ignoring the game. Andy speaks in a low voice. "My professor okayed your cold case for my term project. He warned it could come to nothing and that we shouldn't get our hopes up. He also cautioned me against helping you settle a grudge." I meet his gaze, saying nothing. I will not deny I want to see my parents' murderers get what they deserve. "Okay, I understand." Andy nods. Silent for a minute, while looking at me, he draws out his words. "Pedro. I'll take this on if we agree on one thing."

"What?"

"That we do everything together. We don't go off on our own if we find a fresh clue. Agreed?" Andy holds up his fist for affirmation.

"Agreed." Sealed with a fist bump.

"Okay. Let's go to work. What did you bring?" Andy takes out his camera.

"Here?" It's halftime and the skybox has emptied. Shrugging, I begin pulling out my most personal belongings, setting them on the table.

"Here's a photo of my parents. You can have it for now. It's a duplicate. This is the newspaper story about their death. This is my mother's cross. I don't know what happened to the heavy gold chain it was hanging on. Stolen maybe." I lay her gold cross on the table. It has an open channel running down the center.

Andy bends his head and peers at it. "Is that dirt along the center channel there?" He points with the tip of a closed pen. I move to pick it up, but Andy grabs my hand away. "Don't touch it. Was your mother wearing this cross the day she was killed?" His voice is louder this time.

"Yes, she never took it off. Why?" Leaning in, I inspect it, too.

"The long part of the cross has black stuff in it. That could be paint from the car that hit them." Andy photographs it, then pulls a glass vial out of his case. With a pair of long tweezers, he places the cross into it. "Don't worry, Pedro. I'll take excellent care of this. It'll be reintroduced as evidence. They'll hold it at the police station in Hialeah until the case is solved or closed. It will be locked up and safe. Is that alright with you?"

"It has to be if it will help the case."

"I wouldn't ask if I didn't think it would. What else do you have?"

"This is an earring my mom was wearing when she died. They never found the other one." Andy takes a close-up photo of it, then puts it into another vial, marking it "Mrs. Ramirez." He writes Mommy's name plus the date and time of her death. I cock my head and meet his eyes. Andy smiles. He has done his homework and knows the details of this case. He then examines both their death certificates, making notes in his journal.

When he finishes, I hand him the heat sheets I purchased at Friday's meet. I know I'm talking too fast as I describe their significance. "I recognized a man in the crowd. Callahan is a high school in Hialeah. I walked over to take a closer look. I was positive he was the owner of the house my dad and I were working on the day Poppy died. I had Luke take a photo with his phone. I sent it to you last night. Did you get it?"

"The two sweaty guys in black jackets?" He brings the image up on his phone.

"Yeah. I watched them for the rest of the meet. At least until they left. They left early. I'm almost positive they were cheering for a swimmer named Justin Espinoza. The house my dad and I were working on was owned by that guy. We used a spigot on the side of the house to fill the wheelbarrow. It was beneath a window, and we saw a lab set up inside. That man..." I touch the image. "He was in the room and saw us. He came outside screaming, telling us to leave. We picked up Poppy's tools and the empty mortar powder bags. On the way out, we opened the garbage bin to dispose of the bags. The bin was three quarters full of battery wrappers."

"Meth lab." Andy's voice is flat.

"That's exactly what my dad told my mom. That evening, Jose and I came home from a pickup game of basketball. A police car with the engine running sat in the driveway. The cop got out and told us our mother and father had been killed." I look away, my eyes filling with tears.

"Pedro, I promise to do everything I can to help find the men responsible for this." Andy speaks with passion and conviction. I believe him.

The skybox fills up for the second half of the game. Tucking my treasured items away, I watch as Andy sits in silence. After a few minutes, he speaks. "Okay, here's where we go from here. I'll meet with the detective who handled this investigation. I'll need to re-examine every piece of evidence as well as present this fresh evidence. We'll run an analysis to discover if the matter embedded in your mother's cross is paint from the automobile that struck her. This week I'll find any information I can about Justin Espinoza and his family. You say you know where the meth house is?"

"Yes."

"We'll take a side trip next Saturday when you guys come to Miami for the game. Hialeah is twenty minutes away. We can look around. For today, can we keep our project just between the two of us? That will keep opinions to a minimum." He's speaking in a low voice so no one else will hear.

I nod, elated at Andy's plan and take-charge approach. "Perfect. Sara knows a little but not much. I won't tell her any more."

"Why are you two so serious over there? Come on! Cheer your team to victory, Andy," Doc booms. "The score's been tied for the last quarter. They need you, son! Wahoo! Will you look at that, Dana? Our little Sara has a game day hat. Very sporty, little lady!"

"Why thank you, Doc." Sara walks in and spins around, her long green skirt billowing out. Danny follows her with Luke and Cheree. Time to get serious about the game and food for the second half. The Hurricanes pull ahead in the last three minutes.

Filing out of the skybox to head for home, I glance at the bottles of liquor on the counter. This time they don't tempt me, don't pull me into the dreaded darkness. I look back a second time just to be sure. Nope, no desire. Thank you, Jesus—and Andy.

7

Chat

I close my Spanish textbook, repeating the verb conjugations out loud that I need to memorize for my test tomorrow morning. My text notification blinks.

Andy: MET WITH THE DETECTIVE ON YOUR PARENTS' CASE TODAY. DETECTIVE ANDECKER.

Me: NEVER MET HIM.

Andy: YEAH, HE'S REOPENING THE FILE.

Me: JUST LIKE THAT?

Andy: HE WAS RELUCTANT. I HAD MY PROFESSOR SEND AN OFFICIAL REQUEST. ANDECKER SOUNDED DEFENSIVE ABOUT THE PAINT SAMPLE. SAID LOTS OF CARS HAD THAT SAME PAINT. HE AGREED TO RUN THE TEST FOR US.

Me: THEN WHAT?

Andy: WE CAN RUN A FEW CROSS-SEARCHES.

Me: ?

Andy: WHATEVER AUTOMOBILE MAKE WE COME UP WITH CROSSED WITH THE ADDRESS OF THAT HOUSE IN HIALEAH. IT'S A LONG SHOT BUT WORTH PURSUING.

Me: WHATEVER IT TAKES. I'LL BET THIS GUY MADE A LOT OF MONEY AND HOOKED A LOT OF KIDS WITH THAT POISON THEY WERE MAKING. AND TO KILL MY PARENTS IN COLD BLOOD OVER IT.

Andy: SOME SICK PEOPLE OUT THERE.

Me: GOT THAT RIGHT.

Andy: Gotta go get some studying done. Later.

Me: Just finished up. Thanks, Andy.

Andy: Sure.

Packing up my books, I sit down to watch TV with Mr. and Mrs. Addison and Jose. Our favorite program is on tonight. Jose snuggles between "Dad and Mom," looking content. It's good to have parents to share stuff with again. True, we're still getting to know each other, but a positive feeling is growing between us. Jose is his old smiling self again, while I'm caught in the past. But only till I know Mommy and Poppy's killers are in prison. Then I'll plan my future ... volunteer for a community art project ... maybe even find a girl to hang out with.

8

Revenge Fantasy

Friday night I rush into the house, in a hurry to get back on the computer.

Our swim meet was at the Boca High pool this week and ran until 9:30. The family is going out for pie, celebrating our second win of the season. Wanting to connect with Andy about our Miami plans tomorrow, I asked to be dropped off at home. As I'm waiting, the computer comes to life. I tap my fingers on the mousepad.

Three emails. One from a girl I'd given my address to in case she needed help with algebra this weekend.

Two from Andy: Dude, I have all the info we need for this weekend. It was in the police files. The address is in Hialeah. Google it. See if it looks like the same house your dad took you to.

The second one reads, "The paint sample from your mom's cross matches that of a midnight blue 2017 BMW 325I series. We have a vehicle to look for."

Why can't it be Saturday already? Hopping up from the chair, I begin pacing. If I sleep tonight, it'll be a miracle. Thank you, Andy! This is way more info than I could have dug up on my own. Quality info. Information we need to send that guy to the big house. Andy is my own personal P.I. Sitting back at the computer, I begin the address search on Google Maps. I check the street view. It's the same house!

Me: Hey, Andy, it looks like you've been busy. Good info. That's definitely the house. The garage in back is the one my dad was building. Looks like they never finished it. Can't make out the car in the drive.

Waiting for a text back, I tip back in my chair, staring at the ceiling. How do we find out who lives there? Park near the house and watch who comes and goes? On TV, how do they do a reverse search on addresses to get the homeowner's name? I began keying in *reverse search ... address lookup*. After ten minutes, I shove the mouse away, frustrated. When I get a hit, the next screen asks for a credit card number. Too many dead ends.

What else? What else? Wait! Did Espinoza do this alone? No way. Was that other guy at the swim meet his partner in crime? Pounding my fist on the table, I sit back in the chair again, trying to remember that last day with Poppy. Fragmented images run through my mind. I need to tell Andy there were two men in the crack house. Possibly the same two men who ran Mommy and Poppy down?

If caught, they both have a lot to lose. Espinoza saw me. Those cold brown eyes—sinister even. Why did he let me live? I shiver, wrapping my arms around my middle. He messed up our lives forever, flushing us down the hole of a foster care system with too many kids. Was that his way of dealing with Jose and me? He probably thought I'd never piece this puzzle together, being only fifteen at the time.

I'll run all this by Andy tomorrow. I get up and pace again. What to do until everyone gets home? Ah, yes! Another seek and kill game. Maybe I can up my score tonight. Now that I have a name for my victim, I'll crush this frustration by gunning down these computer-generated bad guys. So hooked on this stuff!

An hour later, I glance out the window to see headlights bouncing towards the house. Probably Mr. and Mrs. Addison. I'm sure they won't approve of my newfound interest in internet sniper games. I shut down the computer and head upstairs before they come into the house. Pulse racing, I grasp the handrail, taking the steps three at a time. Too charged up to carry on pleasant family talk, I make it to my bedroom before the front door opens. Falling on the bed, face up, I stare at the ever-present swaying shadow of the palm tree on the ceiling.

Jose comes in and turns on the light. Blinking, I sit up on the bed. His cheeks are flushed, and he has a big smile on his face. "Hey, little brother, what's the big smiley face all about?"

"I ate three pieces of pie! Chocolate, lemon meringue, and apple. With ice cream. I'm so full. And now I get to take a hot shower. Pedro, you should have come with us. Why didn't you?"

"The first week of school kinda wore me out, I guess." No way am I wiping that smile off his face. Not with these dark thoughts taking over my mind.

"Yeah, school is hard. Especially after being out for so many months. Mrs. A. is a good teacher. She makes my lessons seem easy. But, Pedro, it's the weekend. You need to go out and have some fun. Eat some pie." Jose laughs, shoving his shoulder into my chest, knocking me off the bed, trying to wrestle me to the floor like he did when we were kids. I let him win for a few minutes then roll over on him and pin him, pumping my fist in the air. "Ganador!"

We turn as Luke comes into our room. "I heard all the pounding up here. What's going on? What's Ganador?"

"It means 'the winner.' Luke, help. He's got me pinned and I can't move." Jose laughs.

Luke hesitates for a quick second. "So, this is what it's going to be like having two brothers? Game on, dudes." Grinning, he comes at me for a full body hit.

"Hey, no fair. Two on one." Now I'm breathing heavy. Luke is my size but has that slender swimmer's build. Still, he's strong. Jose rolls away from us, jumping on the bed, calling out moves. Luke and I laugh and grunt as we each pin then wrestle away from the other.

"Stop!" Sara's standing at the door, looking scared. "Why are you two fighting?"

Luke and I get up. I hang my arm around his shoulder. "We're just goofing off, Sara. No worries."

"Yeah. Like brothers." Luke turns to me. "To be continued." He fist bumps me.

"Mom brought you a piece of pie, Pedro. Apple. It's still warm. It's on the kitchen counter." Sara turns, motioning for me to follow.

"Yum!" In four strides, I'm right behind her. "I worked up an appetite, working these guys over."

I take my pie into the den. Luke puts on a surf video, and Jose immediately falls asleep on the floor cushions. Luke and Sara are texting—Cheree and Danny, probably. My thoughts wander off to tomorrow with Andy. Back to Hialeah. Back to where it all started. I can do this.

9

For Sale

Sara pokes me in the ribs with her elbow. We're in the front seat of Danny's car on our way to Miami. "Why so quiet? You okay?"

"Yeah, great. I love Saturday game days."

"I sometimes wonder what you're thinking when we're riding to Miami." Having nothing to say to that, I look over at her, giving a friendly poke back. Is it because I'm quieter than the others that Sara wonders what's going on in my head? She's a good friend and a good sister.

"I'll never live in Miami again. I forgot how crowded it is. I like the Boca life."

"Well, Boca likes you, too. And so does that girl, Carmen. What's going on?" she teases. "Should we invite her one Saturday?"

"No. Nothing's going on," I'm quick to answer. This is no time for a girl to tag along. I have serious matters to tend to. It's good Luke and Sara are so involved with Danny and Cheree. That gives Andy and me the freedom we need to work on the case. I hope nobody notices our disappearing act today.

At the stadium, Danny pulls into the VIP lane. "Perks of having both parents as alums." He grins, holding up his parking pass. The attendant waves us through. "There's Andy. He's waving us over." No matter how long it's been since Danny last saw his big bro, he's always excited to see him. Just like Jose and me.

Danny hops out and gives Andy a hug. "Hey, Andy! Missed ya, bro."

"Missed you, too, Danny-boy." Andy laughs, greeting the rest of us. "If you hustle, you'll make it in time for kick-off. I need to run back to my place for a seat cushion for Mom. Hey, Pedro, do you want to ride with me?"

"Sure." I get into Andy's old camouflage green and tan Jeep.

"Later." Danny waves as we circle around and drive off.

"That was a smooth exit." I laugh, relaxing into the seat.

"I have to swing by my house and get my mom a cushion—on the way back from Hialeah. How are you doing?" Andy looks over at me.

"Good, good. I guess. I had some rough moments last night. I won't lie. Revenge has been on my mind for a long time, Andy. It seems as if we're getting close to nailing this Espinoza guy." I study him. His cheerful mood is replaced with a deep frown, and he's chewing his bottom lip, and brakes. I assure him, "Don't worry. I won't do anything dumb. I won't go solo, do something on my own. I will totally honor our agreement."

"That's good, Pedro. If I even suspected you'd go rogue, I'd have to report you to the Hialeah police, bro. We don't need that kind of trouble. That isn't what this is about for us. Right?" Andy turns and stares me straight in the eye. I nod. He then accelerates the Jeep onto the highway.

"Right. When I used to get worked up, I'd take a swallow from Big Dee's rum bottle or finish off the last of his bottle after he passed out. He never knew the difference. Last night I wished the Addisons had something strong to drink. They don't keep liquor in the house. I guess that's a good thing." I sure am talking a bunch. Andy is easy to talk to. I don't connect with many people. This feels good.

"Rum and rage. A toxic combo. Back to the task at hand. Would you bring up the Hialeah address on your phone?"

"Sure." Bringing up the map, I show it to him.

"Got it. The case of your parents' death is getting more puzzling every day. I'm discovering lots of clues to follow up on. The trick is uncovering them in the proper sequence."

"Such as?"

"In a hit and run, the correct identification of the automobile is crucial. Once you have a VIN, which is the twenty-digit Vehicle Identification Number, then you can locate the auto. With a hit and run, the car is the murder weapon. Once we find it, we can attach a name to who was operating it."

"What? Espinoza was operating it. I know!"

"In your mind, Espinoza was driving it. At this early point in the investigation, we must keep our minds open to all possibilities. Think as a cop thinks, Pedro. He could have hired someone to do it. There are many scenarios that could have caused your parents' death. Don't worry. We'll find the person responsible."

"I hear what you're saying. We're almost there." Remaining calm takes a huge effort. Andy turns onto a palm tree-lined street. The houses are typical two-story Hialeah houses, square, with flat roofs and large porches and patios. This neighborhood has eight-foot-high fichus hedges surrounding each property. People from Cuba and South America have added the heavy iron bars over the windows, a common design in those countries.

"Nice neighborhood. Crack dealers must make a lot of cash these days," Andy says. "Look for the house number painted on the curb. Houses ending in even numbers are on the east side of the street in Miami." Andy drives slowly. The worn and peeled house numbers are difficult to make out.

"There! That's the house. I recognize it as clear as if it were yesterday. Look! A For Sale sign in the lawn."

"We'll park the car a couple of blocks away and walk back. A neighbor might tell us about the house. We'll act like interested homebuyers. I was with my parents when they were looking for our house in Boca. Hmm, trying to recall the questions they asked the realtors."

"How many bedrooms and bathrooms? How much? Where are the owners moving?" I suggest.

"That's a good start." Andy maneuvers the Jeep into a Mini Mart lot. "I expected a more run-down area. This is a peaceful family neighbor-hood." We round the corner and walk slowly toward the house.

"I guess crack dealers can operate anywhere."

"It doesn't take much physical space to make that poison. Here, I'll call the realtor." We stand in front of the For Sale sign while Andy taps in the number. The still-unfinished garage takes me back eighteen months. The garage door is open, a powder blue Mercedes convertible parked inside. Is anyone home? The place across the street looks like a boarding house, the green lawn replaced by a cement driveway with five cars parked in it. Next to it is a small city park with a basketball court.

"Marcos Avila? Hi, my name is Andy and I'm standing in front of your listing on 122nd Street in Hialeah." He listens for a few moments. "No, just curious. How much? How many bedrooms? Is it occupied now? Whatever you can tell me." He winks at me, sounding official.

Walking up and down on the sidewalk, Andy looks the house over as the realtor speaks. A wide smile crosses his face as he turns to me and stops, giving a thumbs-up. "Okay. You've been a real help. No. I'll call back for an appointment if I want to see the inside. Bye." I can see he's excited because he's bouncing from foot to foot. Soon he hangs up, shoving his phone into his pocket.

Grabbing my elbow and turning me, he guides me back toward the Mini Mart. "Wow! Good info, Pedro. Here's the deal. It's a divorce sale. The husband was running his business out of their home and the wife booted him out. She's living there with the son, who goes to high school. Callahan High. That's the public high school for this neighborhood."

"Told you! Espinoza! What else did he say?"

"Right now, the boy and his mother are living here until the house sells. The dad is living in Boca, running his business there. The son stays with the dad on weekends. That real estate agent must be new. He shared their private information like it was his to tell. I wonder who's getting the BMW in the divorce. It's not here, and that powder blue Mercedes is most likely a woman's car," Andy says.

Just like in the cop shows we watch! Excitement building, heart beating faster, I answer, "We're hot on his trail now."

"Not really. In fact, our trail may have just gone ice cold. If Espinoza is renting, or living with friends in Boca, we may have lost him. For now. There won't be phone or Florida Power and Light records to search. Realtors aren't allowed to reveal any information about their clients either. That dude sure let a lot of info slip. We know a lot more than we did five minutes ago." I go silent, turning over this recent information. "Hey, we'll find this guy, Pedro. It may take longer than we thought. We still need to examine the original police report, paint samples, and the VIN number. If all else fails, we'll go to the next swim meet when you guys compete against Callahan."

"Yeah, I guess." Combing my fingers through my hair, I tuck it tight behind my ears.

"Pedro, we've hardly started our detective work. These cold cases take time and legwork." On our trip back into Miami, Andy stops in front of a small, coral colored apartment house. "Be right back."

10

Game Face

Waiting in Andy's Jeep, I go over what we've learned in the last hour. Yeah, it's a start. But what's next? It's all so complicated. Still energized, I begin cracking my knuckles while looking around the Jeep. What's that? Between the seats, half covered with a notebook, is an open pack of smokes.

Andy returns with a green and orange UM stadium pad. "Can't come back empty-handed." He grins.

Working up the courage to ask him about the cigarettes, I say, "Hey, Andy, do you smoke?" I gesture down.

"Busted. I like to smoke when I drive long distances. Like from Miami to Boca and back. But please don't tell anyone. With both parents being doctors, it's nothing I advertise."

"I won't. I smoked when I lived in the circus. I'm going through withdrawal. Could I bum one or two off you?" I hold my breath while biting my lower lip. Am I asking too much? Will he understand?

"No worries. Take what you need. It'll be our secret." I let out my breath, opening the top of the small box. The warning "SMOKING KILLS" takes up the bottom half of the pack. I light one up and inhale. The smoke hits my lungs big time. I cough, wiping my wet eyes. Andy glances sideways at me. Rookie move. I'll go easier with the rest of the cigarette.

"I don't know if I could do this kind of work, Andy. So much can change in a year."

"Some of the cases other students are working on are thirty years old. That's the fun—and the challenge of it. You, Pedro, are emotionally attached to the outcome of this case. That's what makes it so tough for you. It's written all over your face."

"True, true. I'm sure it'll get easier." Glancing out the window, I avoid meeting his eyes. Is my face that easy to read? I won't be a pretender when it comes to honoring my love for Mommy and Poppy. This is the only way I know.

Soon, Andy steers the Jeep into the stadium parking lot. "Time to put your game face on, Pedro. This is a big game for UM. We need all the team spirit we can get." The noise of cheering crowds erupts from the stadium. "I grew up going to football games every Saturday. It was a blast! Loosen up and enjoy the day." Andy sounds excited. We quicken our steps up the stairs to the skybox.

He puts his arm around my shoulder, steering me into the skybox. "We're here!" he announces, setting the pad on his mother's chair.

"Let the party begin!" Doc booms. He passes us each a burger, picking the last one up for himself. "Don't be shy. Serve yourself whatever you want, Pedro." We ate gigantic beef burgers, watching as UM was losing badly to Vanderbilt.

In the middle of the fourth quarter, two of Andy's friends drop by. One of them calls out, "Hey, Doc! If you've won five national championships but no students or players at your school are alive to remember any of them, did they actually happen?" We have a great laugh at Doc's expense.

Andy says, "See you all later. I don't need to watch this humiliation. Oh, I forgot to tell you. Next weekend I'll be in Boca."

"Why don't you ride up Friday and watch Sara dive?" Danny asks. "We have a home meet against a couple of schools from Miami. What schools, Sara? Do you remember?"

"Callahan and Kendall," Sara says.

"I'll be there for sure!" Andy waves goodbye, slightly raising his eyebrows, giving me a small nod. Soon the skybox empties. Strolling over to the bar, I open a cola. The bottles of liquor underneath the counter are calling to me. I glance around. I'm alone. That familiar black mood sucks me in once again. Opening my backpack, I slip a full, unopened bottle of rum into it.

The open bottle of rum on the counter is tempting me beyond my strength. Unscrewing the cap, I empty the amber liquid into my can. The smell of rum hits my nose, and I nearly gag. So glad the cola masks the taste. I return the bottle to its place when Danny and Sara come through the door, holding hands. They're having fun in their own world. Fun I hope to have someday, too. I'm tired of feeling isolated and alone—and so out there. The loneliness, a physical ache in my chest. Taking a deep breath, I shake it off, chugging from the can.

The desired effect comes quickly. "Looks as if we lost our first game of the season." I smile, a giddy sensation flooding my body. I want to feel normal, too ... like everybody else.

"Yeah, the first loss always hurts. Let's try to beat the crowd out of the parking lot," Danny suggests. "Has anybody seen Luke and Cheree?" Danny again takes Sara's hand, who catches mine. We bump into them on the way out. After saying our goodbyes, we begin the long trip home. I doze on and off the entire way.

Entering Boca, we pass Atkins New and Used Autos. The lot is jammed with customers.

"Keep driving, keep driving," Cheree says. "I don't need my parents to see that I'm back. They'll want me to come in to work. These Cash 4 Clunkers customers are super high maintenance. Not your everyday tire-kicker type consumers. It's a buying frenzy."

"I didn't realize there were so many people with clunkers." Luke laughs. "I thought Danny was the only one!"

"Ha ha. At least I have wheels. More trash talk like that and it will be Cash 2 Ride for you, bro," Danny jokes.

"That's the point," Cheree replies. "These people aren't just bringing in clunkers. Some are bringing in perfectly good cars only a couple of years old! *Greedy people* is what I'm saying! They just want a new car, compliments of the US Government."

"I'm hungry. Who wants to go eat?" Danny asks.

"There's nobody home at my house. We can raid the takeout boxes in the refrigerator," Cheree offers.

"Hey, could you drop me off at home?" I ask. "I'd be a real fifth wheel. If you know what I mean!"

"Never, Pedro! But I get it." Danny grins.

"Thanks. Besides, you guys won't miss me." I elbow Sara, who giggles. My date is with a bottle of rum and the computer.

11

Wednesday Night

Wednesday evenings are great because we stay busy. Luke and Sara go straight from swim and dive practice to church, picking Jose and I up on the way. We go early so Sara can get ready for her song set and help with the sound check. She's teaching me how to operate the soundboard. Danny and I go to the church kitchen to finish our homework before the service.

"Danny! Hi!" It's Danny's little buddy from Vacation Bible School, Ray Ray, sounding excited to see Danny. "I missed you! What're you reading?" He climbs onto the chair next to Danny's, looking at the pictures in his earth science book.

"I'm reading about Planet Earth. It's an amazing place. Look, this volcano in Costa Rica has fire running down the slopes." Danny points to fire lining a mountainside.

"Wow, that's cool!" Five-year-old Ray Ray slips his arm around Danny's neck. "Did you know God created the earth in six days? He was tired on the seventh day and took a nap."

"I remember reading that," Danny says.

"Danny, did you finish reading Luke?" Ray Ray asks, his eyes wide as he looks at Danny.

"Yes, and I paid special attention to the red words, just like you said. Listen... Do you hear that?" Danny asks. They look at each other as Ray Ray claps his hands, obviously recognizing Sara's clear voice.

"Sara," Ray Ray whispers reverently, his eyes getting big as he looks from Danny to me. He jumps off the chair. "Let's go watch her sing."

"Hey, I know a special place. If I take you there, will you promise not to tell anyone?" Danny sounds mysterious.

"Yeah. And I can be really quiet, too," the little guy promises. Danny takes his hand. Walking to the front of the church, we find a narrow flight of stairs. At the top, a small balcony faces the altar.

"Wow!" Ray Ray breathes, his face glowing. When the song ends, he announces, "I'm going to ask Sara to marry me. I love her."

"Hmm!" Danny says. "She is lovable, isn't she? Sara loves you, too. What would happen if I asked her first? Would we still be friends?"

"Well, since you're older than me, that would be ... okay," Ray Ray says, drawing the last part out as if deep in thought. "Look, she sees us up here!" Waving with both arms over his head, he points to Danny and me. Giving us her Sara smile, she nods as she counts off the opening beats to the next song.

"Did you know Sara babysits me and my baby sister?"

"No, I didn't," Danny answers. "There's a lot about Sara I don't know."

"My mom and dad go bowling every Tuesday night. It starts pretty soon. I always help Sara with her homework. She doesn't like to study much."

"It's good that you help her, Ray Ray. Homework is important," I say. "I help her too."

"We should get back. Mommy will worry," the little boy says, taking Danny's hand, leading us to the stairs. Danny turns. Sara is smiling up at him. She's standing there, the purple spotlight highlighting her mass of dark wavy hair, and I can tell by his smile he knows he's a lucky dude.

"Whew! She could be the one. Never thought I'd say that at this age." He shakes his head as if to clear it.

"Seems she has you in her sights, too, bro. You're one fortunate guy." We follow Ray Ray down the stairs.

"Yeah, but what should I do? Sara is different from other girls. I'd hate to blow it by doing something stupid." Danny shakes his head again. "My whole life is totally different these days. I'm learning and doing things that actually matter. Like faith and Bible study. I'm too busy to just hang out and meet girls at the beach the way I did last summer. This is better," he says. "Not that I understand the Bible and all. It's important to Sara. So, it's becoming important to me."

"Sounds like you got it bad, Danny." I grin. "I say ... go for it."

Rounding the corner, we nearly collide with Luke and Cheree. "Hey! What's up?" Luke asks.

"We were just listening to the band rehearse. Me, Pedro, and the Dude here," Danny says.

"Double R! high-five!" Luke holds up a hand, and Ray Ray struggles to reach it.

"Hi, Ray Ray. You're in my class tonight. Do you want me to take you there? We're measuring you guys for costumes." Cheree helped Sara out with Vacation Bible School a few weeks ago. After that, Cheree volunteered for the childcare ministry during the midweek service.

"How's your class going, Cheree?" I ask.

"Pretty good. At first, I didn't think I could handle the craziness ten children can create. Now, I look forward to it all day," Cheree says in her quiet voice. "They're practicing for the Christmas play and I'm thrilled. I go to The School of Performing Arts, and my dream is to become a set designer. It seems as if my first production has fallen right into my lap. And Ray Ray is going to play Joseph, who is married to Mary." She turns to Ray Ray.

"I get to be Joseph!" he announces importantly. "I get to walk around with a donkey and Andrea sitting on it. She's Mary. I hope she doesn't fall off." Ray Ray tries to wink, but in the effort, ends up squeezing both eyes shut. He keeps trying, with the same results, while we laugh.

Cheree says, "We'd better get to class." Taking Ray Ray's hand, she heads towards her room. "I love this boy!" she mouths to us before rounding the corner and disappearing.

"Let's get a seat. I'm exhausted from swimming," Luke says. Danny's leading the way to seats where there's an unobstructed view of Sara. "Good pick. I can see where your priorities are." I laugh.

"Hey, it's a good view of Pastor Thomas, too."

"Supposed to be big swells coming in at sunrise tomorrow. That would give us about one hour of good surf time before class." Luke looks over at Danny and me.

"I'll be by at 5:00 to pick you guys up. I could use some chill time out on the water. And if we don't make it back in time for first period?" Danny asks.

"Then we don't make it back in time for first period," Luke says. "No girls?"

"No girls."

"Glad we had this conversation." We chuck fists. The lights go down, and the band begins their first song. Jose slips in next to me, and I put my arm around his shoulders. Thank you, Father, for rescuing us from Big Dee and keeping us together. This feels good. Tonight, I'm more connected to this new life and family.

Pastor Thomas gave Danny, Jose, and me each a new teen Bible. Reading it was turning out to be more complex than I thought it would be. I attacked it as I would any textbook. But it didn't read like a textbook ... or fiction ... or nonfiction ... or anything I'd ever studied before. Tracking down Pastor Thomas, I tell him of my confusion.

"Good. Now we have a starting point!" Then Pastor gives me a chart about how to read the Bible in chronological order. "Connect with Jonas Friend, our high school youth leader."

Thoughts of Pastor's message on the Bible verse, Psalm 10:18 echo in my mind. "You will bring justice to the orphans and the oppressed, so mere people can no longer terrify them."

This message of hope settles me the more I consider it. God brought justice to Jose and me, as orphans and oppressed by Big Dee. He rescued us from that life by bringing us to the Addisons, who took us in, no questions asked. They protected us from Dee and the media, who were after us, terrorizing Jose and me.

The shadows of the palm tree on the ceiling bring peace tonight. Sleep comes easily.

12

BMW Hunting

My knee bounces while sitting through the last minutes of class. Will Espinoza come to the swim meet tonight? If so, what can we do? This class is dragging by. The hands on the clock over the door are barely moving. I look out the window. Yes! The yellow school buses bringing the Callahan swim team are pulling into the pool parking lot. My heart begins hammering, I glance around. Does anybody notice my excitement?

Andy texted that he'd be riding up from Miami and that traffic was light for a Friday afternoon. It's coming together—finally. I push my way out of the classroom door before the dismissal bell finishes ringing.

The Addison's and Danny's parents show up at the pool at 7:00. We sit in the Addison's' usual spot, watching the Boca swimmers warm up. I'm half paying attention to the conversations going on around me. I jerk back to the present when Mr. Addison puts his arm around my shoulders and says, "Now, Pedro here is extremely focused. He has earned A's in every subject. He's considering studying forensic science, like Andy. Fascinating work!"

I grin, again searching the crowd across the pool for Espinoza. So far, I can't locate him. Justin Espinoza is here, or at least his name is on my heat sheets. It's still early. It just feels later because it's getting dark so much earlier and the fall weather is cooler.

"Absolutely!" Doc glances toward the pool entrance. "Andy loves it. He should be here shortly. Said he'd come by to watch Sara dive." My phone vibrates in my pocket. Tapping it, I read a text from Andy: Meet me in the parking lot. Let's go BMW hunting.

"He just texted me that he's in the parking lot. I'll go get him." I take the bleacher steps two at a time.

I find Andy, and we walk up and down the rows of trucks, SUVs, and cars in search of a midnight blue BMW. "I have the original police report," Andy says. "It's standard, the usual jargon. I didn't spot anything we could use. It was as if they weren't interested in identifying the hit and run driver at all. Just a brief report by Detective Andecker. The single working clue we have is the paint sample from your mom's cross. How they missed that, I'll never know. Sloppy police work."

"I don't see any BMWs, much less a midnight blue one. Let's hang out near the front gate. We can check out the cars as they come in," I reply. "According to the heat sheets, Justin Espinoza doesn't swim until the second half of the meet. That's when Sara dives, too. We have plenty of time."

"Good idea," Andy sits on a large orange plastic barrier near the entrance. I join him. Cars are streaming into the brightly lit parking lot. In the distance, the announcer signals the opposing teams to begin their warm-ups. A few minutes later, Cheree drives up in her Mustang, looking frustrated. Who could be frustrated driving around in a car like that?

"Hi, you guys. Did you save a spot for me?" she jokes, looking around in dismay at the packed parking lot.

"Sure. We can move these barriers, and you can park right here." Andy pulls the one he was sitting on aside to form an extra parking space. We direct her so she can fit her car into the tight spot.

"How come you're so late?" I open the door for her.

"This stupid Cash 4 Clunkers trade-in deal. People keep coming into my dad's dealership and asking all kinds of questions. We're packed with car buyers. It's been that way all week. Finally, I told my mom and dad I was taking off or I'd miss Luke's event. They're closing soon anyhow. What're you guys doing out here?"

"We're watching out for a dude with a midnight blue BMW. His name is Espinoza," Andy answers, looking around.

Cheree snorts. "Well, you won't find that guy in a BMW anymore. He traded it in for a brand-new black Ford Crown Vic yesterday. Is he a buddy of yours?"

I stare at her. "What?" Did I hear her right? "No, not a friend."

"Good! Because that guy's a real creep. A solid sleaze ball liar if you ask me. The car had clearly been in a front-end collision, but he continued to deny it. He worked that lie hard to get as much cash as he could out of my dad. My dad was ready to tell him to take a hike. So, he finally came clean. He said a cousin had borrowed the car and crashed into a fence, just a fender bender. He eventually accepted the trade-in amount my dad was offering and rode off in his new car."

"Cheree, where's the BMW today?" Andy's voice is tense.

"It's in the back lot with the rest of the clunkers. Monday, they'll stack them up on the car carriers and ship them out. Where to, I don't know. Good riddance!"

"What time does your dad get to work in the morning?" Andy asks.

"He'll be in around 6:00. Sadly, so will I. Don't look now, but there's Espinoza pulling into the lot in his new Crown Vic. Compliments of US taxpayers." Cheree tips her head toward the front gate. "I'm getting out of here before he sees me. Thanks for the parking spot. Later." She disappears into the crowd.

Andy and I look at each other. Did this just happen? In one chance conversation, we have access to the BMW and Espinoza. "Wow! We just hit the jackpot." Andy pulls his phone out of his pocket. "I need to call my professor before we do anything. If we do the wrong thing, we could blow it by tainting the evidence. Keep an eye on Espinoza."

"Don't worry. I'm not letting him out of my sight. He's on his phone. The Vic's engine is still running. I need to get out of sight, too, in case he recognizes me."

"Let's get into the Jeep. He might decide to take off." Andy leads the way. I listen as he leaves an urgent message with details of the recent development for his professor.

"I'm sure Espinoza wants to watch his son swim."

"Not all parents are like the Addison's, Pedro. Especially those who conduct their illegal drug deals out of their homes and cars."

"Right. Forgot about that." We sit slouched down in Andy's Jeep, watching and waiting. Espinoza's headlights go on and he takes off toward the exit. Andy starts the Jeep and follows at a distance. Espinoza pulls onto the street in front of the school, then pulls over onto the grass and parks. Andy jerks his steering wheel to stay inside the parking lot. He circles, as if searching for a parking spot. Spotting one near the fence that runs along the street, he pulls in, and we watch the Crown Vic. Even though I don't think Espinoza can see me, I stay hunched down in my seat.

A dark car with tinted windows brakes beside Espinoza. Andy snatches his phone and starts recording video. "Write down the license plate numbers!" The second car speeds off, and two minutes later, a second car pulls up. Sweating, Andy records more video as I write down the license plates, makes, and models of the cars.

"This guy is beyond stupid. Peddling drugs on school property is an instant prison sentence. If we don't get him one way, Pedro, we'll get him for this. Stay still, Pedro. These thugs carry big guns. You know from experience they don't hesitate to kill." Ten minutes later, the Crown Vic pulls away, driving off toward the highway.

"I feel bad for his kid. His old man prefers doing dope deals to watching him compete." The taste in my mouth turns bitter. "Should we follow him ... find out where he lives?"

"I thought about that. We can pick up his contact information from the Atkins Dealership tomorrow. I don't want to do anything until I hear from my professor." Just then, Andy's phone vibrates. "Hi, Pops. Yeah, he's here with me. Okay, we'll be right there." Andy turns to me. "Sara's about to dive, and Luke is getting ready to swim."

I check my heat sheet. "Justin swims right after Luke. Lane five." We walk onto to the pool deck just in time to cheer Luke on as he swam in lane four. We stay there, waiting for the next heat. Time to get a closer look.

Justin stands tall on the starting block. Latino for sure, medium height, with a swimmer's build, and enough hair to require a swim cap. Wow! What an amazing, thick unibrow! It runs straight across the top of his forehead ... like someone had taken a piece of black charcoal and drew across it with a heavy hand. With my phone camera, I zoom in and grab a quick shot.

Justin swims incredibly fast and cakewalks his event. Pulling himself out of the pool, he looks around, as if searching for his dad. Not locating him, Justin hangs his head, toweling himself off. I feel bad for this kid. Sad for the both of us ... for a reason I can't put into words.

"Let's hang with the families and enjoy the rest of the night," Andy says. "Our work here is done for today."

"Yeah. I suppose." My work will never be finished. Not until Espinoza suffers behind bars. Enjoy the evening? The music and brilliant pool lights, even the BBQ smells from the concession stand, fail to draw me in. Maybe someday. That familiar black feeling envelopes me as I mount the bleachers behind Andy. Blood pounds in my ears. No way can I focus on what's happening around me. I sit next to Jose. Only this keeps me going.

"Do you think you'll join the swim team when you get to high school?" I ask.

"Nope. Baseball. Like Poppy. Look, the high school baseball field is over there." Jose points to the back of the school property. "If you look past the pool scoreboard, you can watch the game from here. The score is tied, 3-3."

I laugh and high-five him. I wonder if Luke has an old glove and ball in the garage. I'll ask tomorrow.

13

Kill Games

Alone in a crowd once again. Pain jabs inside. Fresh. My heart breaking all over again. Nobody ever speaks of Mommy and Poppy—as if they never existed. Tucking my elbows into my sides, I wrap my arms around my stomach, leaning in, hoping to ease the pain. Not working. Taking in a deep breath, I work to pull myself out of this black hole. Swim meets aren't the place to grieve.

Jose and our new family and friends are cheering, laughing, and having a great time. Going through the motions, but not feeling it, I join in. My body's here, but my heart, mind, and soul ... somewhere else. When will I be free of this sudden sadness that comes on without warning? I shudder. Tonight will not end well. Can I get to sleep without a drink of rum? It's been six days... I resisted the temptation. Now this. Watching Espinoza conduct his drug deals at my new school, free as a bird, set me on edge. Staring at the baseball scoreboard in the distance, I pull my hair back behind my ears, tucking it tight.

Later, I lie awake, tracking the palm tree shadow chasing across my ceiling, fighting the fierce desire to take a long drink from the bottle of rum in my bathroom.

After tossing and turning for nearly an hour, I give in. I take the bottle from its hiding place and swallow a mouthful. It tastes like bad medicine. I need the effect it has on my out-of-control thoughts. I take a second swallow. This time it hits hard, the rum burning its way down. I shiver. That's the ticket! Now for some kill time on the computer. My own personal party. My victim tonight is Espinoza. Just some target practice, old man. You'll get yours soon. That's a promise.

Quietly creeping down the flight of stairs and into the den, I turn the computer on. I freeze as the initial three tones blare through the speakers. That's loud! Looking over the top of the monitor, I wait to see if I woke anybody. After a few minutes of silence, I feel safe enough to continue. Plugging the headset in, I adjust it for max comfort and sound.

For the next two hours, I hone my hunt and kill skills. My timing and game levels increase. It's as if I'm weightless, moving around inside the game. Heart racing, I sweat, warmth spreading through my chest. I can do anything during these stolen moments of power!

Three AM ... finally spent ... after slaying the enemy over and over. I'll sleep well tonight. Andy and I have that early morning visit with Cheree's dad.

14

Chief Howell

Luke and Sara silently eat breakfast, waiting for Danny at 6:00. They're ready for a day of surfing and beach volleyball. A day of play. I'll play soon enough—just not today. Mr. A. is reading his Bible at the kitchen table. Helping myself to a bowl of Krazy Krispies, I wait for Andy. Groggy and hung over, I'm still more than ready to get on with Andy's case. My case.

"You're up early." Luke looks over at me. "Are you coming with us?"

"No, Andy's working on a cold case for his master's degree, and he's letting me tag along. This morning we're going to Atkins Dealership to investigate a car he thinks was involved in his case." I look away. I've been told a few times we don't keep secrets in this house. Hopefully, I'll be able to tell them the full truth soon enough.

"Cool," Sara says. "Is it one of those cold cases that's thirty years old or something?"

I laugh. "No, not that old. Unfortunately, I'm sworn to secrecy since it's 'live' police work at this point. I wish I could tell you about it though." Mr. A. glances up at me, one eyebrow slightly raised, tilting his head. Can he tell by my voice how involved I am? I need to keep a closer watch on what I say around the house.

After Sara and Luke leave, I get up and pour myself a cup of coffee. Mr. A. shakes his head at my gesture, offering to pour him a second cup, too. "So, you two are on a top-secret mission? Is it as exciting as our favorite crime investigation show on TV?"

"There's a lot more to it. For example, there are so many more procedures to follow for handling evidence. Plastic bags are never used because of static electricity. They always use glass vials and cardboard boxes for storage. Every piece of evidence must have the date, time, case number, and name with the specific source and location where it was collected. They photograph everything, every step of the way. Everything."

"There wouldn't be time for the story if they did that on TV!" Mr. A. grins. "How soon does Andy expect to complete the case he's working on?"

"I don't know. It's slow going. He texted me earlier that he's required to have a detective from the Boca police force accompany us to Atkins Dealership. In the meantime, the Hia— I mean, the police force where the crime was committed has to be contacted. The Boca Police have to be brought into the case."

Heat crawls up the back of my neck, causing instant sweat. Wiping it away, I tuck my hair behind my ears. Wow! I slipped big time. Did Mr. A. catch it? "Only then can we go over to the dealership and look at the car he needs to see." The words come out too fast.

Mr. A. studies me for a moment, both eyebrows raised this time. "Hialeah?" His voice holds no judgement.

"Yes." I look down, then over at the man who has shown so much faith in me.

"I see. You realize Chief Howell lives right next door. He can help you and Andy better than anyone. I'd feel better about your involvement in a criminal case if Chief were involved."

"Oh, yeah. I forgot about Chief." I look out the window. "He's out there mowing his lawn." At 6:00 AM? That's dedication. "Do you think it would be alright to ask his advice when Andy gets here?"

"Excellent idea! And, Pedro? You can tell me anything. Your instincts are great because of having only yourself to depend on while traveling with the circus. But here, you have a network of people who want to help you. No need is too small. In the meantime, I'll be praying for you and your safety. I love you."

Choking up, I turn and walk to the refrigerator for a cold glass of milk. It has been a long time since a father has offered unconditional love. Whatever this is, it feels solid. Undeserved, for sure, seeing as I now have serious secrets. How does this father-son trust work? Turning, I read the expression on Mr. A.'s face. I just know he's figured out what we're up to. What else does he know? I couldn't bear it if he knew about the drinking, smoking, and gaming. Touching my fingers to my nose, I wonder if the smell like nicotine.

"As soon as I can, I'll explain the case. I promise. Your trust in me is important, sir." I pick up my backpack. "I hear Andy's car in the driveway. We'll check in with Chief before we leave. Thank you for the suggestion."

"Dude, our next door neighbor is Chief Howell, as in the Boca Raton Police Chief Howell. Do you think he could cut through the red tape you're talking about?" Andy's face lights up when I point to, then wave at, Chief. Chief drives his riding lawn mower to where we stand.

After being introduced, Andy tells Chief about his project concerning Mommy and Poppy's cold case. He takes a long time describing the details we've uncovered so far, details I would have skipped. Details, details, details! Police work is tedious. Let's get going to the dealership. Chief takes off his beat-up straw hat, studies me, then swipes his sweaty forehead with his shirtsleeve. He glances toward our house. Turning, I see Mr. A. looking through the window. He gives a slight nod and steps back out of view.

"Mrs. Howell left iced tea and coffeecake on the kitchen table. We should discuss this in the air conditioning. Your case sounds complicated, and we need to calculate how to proceed. I'll call to find out if the report from Hialeah has arrived. They can email it to the house." Chief starts the motor of his lawnmower. "Race ya!" he challenges, laughing as Andy and I easily pass him on the way to the garage.

Inside, we listen as Chief makes a few phone calls. The last one is long, and Chief sounds displeased toward the end. He taps his phone and scowls. "The detective on the case in Hialeah left for vacation this morning. He clipped a note to the report stating that if there were fresh developments, we must wait for his return before proceeding."

"How long will he be gone?" Are we about to hit a brick wall?

"Two weeks," Chief answers. "That is a highly unusual request. They do things oddly down there in South County. I've never heard of a two-week delay to examine evidence of a potential murder weapon."

"Can we call him? Did they say where he is?" Andy suggests.

"He's on a flight to Bogota, Colombia. He and his wife are taking one of those ten-day Caribbean cruises back to Miami. No help there." Chief holds up an enormous chunk of gooey coffeecake. "My wife requests that I only eat one piece of cake. At times, I ignore her requests. I do what I consider necessary." Chief deliberately takes a large bite of the cake, winking at us. "Let's go to the station and pull a search warrant, then call on Kenny Atkins." He crams the rest of the cake into his mouth. Dusting the crumbs off his graying beard, he picks up his bag and leads us out to his police cruiser. I get into the back while Andy sits in front.

"I have a copy of the original police report and paperwork from the case, sir. My professor was able to get it for me since this is a master's level forensic science project," Andy offers.

"Perfect! We'll have all the numbers required to fill in the blanks on the warrant. It's all about the numbers with police paperwork. Have you ever filled out paperwork to get a search warrant, kid?" Andy shakes his head. "Good! I'll show you how it's done. Who knows? Maybe you'll be working with the Boca Police Department someday." Chief looks at me in the rearview mirror. "Pedro, now that you're caged up in my cruiser, I need you to make me a promise."

"Yes, sir?"

"Because it was your parents who were killed, I'm mindful you are emotionally invested in this case. You need to know your place." Chief is stern.

"Sir?"

"As of today, I'm the investigating officer on this case here in Palm Beach County. I'll let you hang around as much as I can. If and when events become dangerous, you must do as I say. Make no mistake about it. I will demand that both of you remain in the safety of your homes if I believe it's necessary. From this point on, you can't touch anything related to the case. Either of you. Agreed?"

"Agreed." As much as I don't like these rules, I know we're in excellent hands.

15

Cash 4 Clunkers

Chief pulls the squad car into the Boca Police station. Passing through the secure areas, we walk straight to his office in the back. Chief's walk is brisk. My steps are slow, as if I'm moving in slow motion. I'm inside a police station. Fear grips my stomach, then passes as fast as it came. Being invisible to cops is a knee-jerk reaction I need to get over. Locating the only door leading in and out of the large office is second nature. Will I always be on the lookout for an escape route?

I'm no longer on the run! I glance around, details grabbing my attention. The room smells fresh—if that's a smell. Uniformed men and women sit at the eight desks: four on each side of the aisle we are walking down to Chief's office. No one pays attention to me as I move down the aisle, the pounding in my ears louder than their voices. This is incredible. I'm free. And I'm with the Chief! Returning to my senses, I step up my pace and join Andy inside Chief's office.

"I must hand it to you two; you have done a fine job flushing out this Espinoza."

"Thanks, Chief. Some of it was just dumb luck. For example, that whole Cash 4 Clunkers situation," Andy says.

"The BMW is now property of the US government. That'll simplify our job in the long run. Before we go, I need to upload the video you filmed last night, Andy. If this Espinoza is the individual who ran Mr.

and Mrs. Ramirez down, there had to have been a powerful motive. If it was drug related, we'll need to prove that." Andy takes his video camera from his backpack.

Chief calls one of the other officers in to copy it. "Have it sent to the lab for a complete description. Make, model, and color of all cars. Plates and the movements of the drivers if possible. Put a rush on it. Here's the case number and name."

Leaning back in my chair, I clasp my hands behind my head and look over at Andy. We grin as Chief takes charge, barking out orders. Even Andy seems impressed at the efficient manner Chief dives in and handles business. He has a search and arrest warrant made out in case we turn up evidence that would incriminate Espinoza. Yes! Things are finally moving along. What a dead end that Hialeah detective turned out to be, stalling the case another two weeks! By then, the BMW would have been long gone.

Within the hour, we're turning into Atkins New and Used Car Dealership. Chief brought along an evidence specialist, Officer Sanchez. We find a parking space around back, near the fenced-in yard of old cars.

"That's it! Over there! The blue BMW." I point.

"First things first. Let's check in with Kenny Atkins." Chief strides over to the side door of a building marked OFFICE. A tall man steps out. "Kenny, how's it going? We're here to gather evidence on a BMW you took in trade. It may be the automobile we're searching for in a hit and run."

"No kidding. I knew that guy wasn't being straight with me. He was one of those fast talking, full-of-hot-air types," Mr. Atkins says. "I'll get the keys. It's scheduled to ship out first thing Monday morning to a holding terminal in Atlanta."

"We may need to take it if it's the car we're looking for. Will that be a problem? It'll be returned to you ultimately, but I can't guarantee the exact date," Chief tells him as we walk over to the car, stopping ten feet away from it.

"No problem, Chief. I'll let you boys do what you do best. Is there anything else I can help you with?" Mr. Atkins asks.

"I'll need the information you have on the seller, including his contact info," Chief says.

"He paid cash for the new Crown Vic. That's rare these days. I'll have my wife copy the file for you." Mr. Atkins leaves. I'm so ready to get under that car and see what I can discover.

"Okay. Officer Sanchez will approach the car and take photos from every angle. I'll do a visual check of the body. Andy, here is the form for the visual. I'll call out the area and description of any damage. Note it in my exact words. Pedro, you just hang tight for now." What? I run my fingers through my hair. How long will this visual check take?

"Let's start with the VIN number." Chief spends the next hour poring over the car from every angle. He calls out tiny details, which Andy writes on the report. Officer Mike photographs each item. He dusts for fingerprints on the door handles. He opens the passenger-side door and begins carefully dusting the interior for further prints.

Chief props open the hood and motions for Andy and I to look inside. Finally! The hood is sticking slightly because of the body damage on the driver's side. I pull on the plastic gloves I got at the station.

Officer Sanchez gets out of the car holding a folded paper with a pair of long tweezers. "This is a receipt for a new windshield. It was stuck between the console and passenger seat." He lays it in an open cardboard box. We read it.

"Look at the date! It's three days after your parents were hit." Andy looks at me. "Check this out. They replaced the windshield at a body shop in Jacksonville. That's curious. If the accident happened in Hialeah, the owner must have had it towed to Jacksonville. That's 600 miles."

"I'm confident there's a story there." Chief draws out his words, returning to examine the engine. "They were hit on the driver's side. That headlight was replaced. The original police report said nothing about a shattered headlight. You can run down the make and model of a car with the broken glass from a headlight. That's just sloppy police work. This entire case is smelling like a three-day-old dead fish," he growls.

I study the VIN number etched into the windshield under the wiper on the driver's side. Something flashes, catching my eye, then is gone. Moving over the area again, I hope to get a glimpse of what it was. There it is again! Something is trapped in the drain under the windshield. "Officer Sanchez, what do you make of this?" I point. "There's something caught in the drain beneath the windshield wipers. Can you see it? It sparkles in the sunlight when you catch it at the right angle."

"There it is. I see it." Officer Sanchez peers into the drainage area with a small flashlight. He pulls out his long tweezers and tries to pry the small object loose. It's wedged in too tightly.

Grunting, Chief scoots under the car to get a better view. "Mike, I have a clear view of the drain from here. If you pry the grill apart, it'll fall right into my hand. Take a picture first. Andy, record the information on the report. Then we'll pry it loose."

"Here goes." The item falls into Chief's hand. He holds it out from under the car for us to see.

"That's my mother's amethyst earring!" I cry out. "She was wearing it the day she was killed!"

"The other one is in the evidence bag in Hialeah. I have a picture," Andy confirms.

"Bingo! It's time I had a chat with Mr. Espinoza. Not too smart, using a government program to ditch the evidence of a double murder," Chief states. "Mike, get the paperwork from Kenny Atkins and meet us at the car." Preoccupied, Chief says, "I'll drop you two off at the Addisons'. As soon as I find out anything new, I'll call you. I'll do my best to get a confession out of this guy. This puts the car at the scene of the murder, thus making it the murder weapon. I don't even need to see if the paint samples match. I'm sure they do!"

Adrenaline pumping, my heart races. Taking a deep breath in, I exhale slowly, wanting more than anything to be in that room when Chief hammers Espinoza with the evidence. I need to see him squirm ... get that trapped look with nowhere to go but prison ... surely a satisfying sight.

The Addison house is empty when Chief drops us off. "I need to write this up while it's fresh in my mind for my project." Andy seems preoccupied with the details of the case again.

Driving off in his Jeep, he leaves me alone with thoughts of a very bloody revenge. A few swallows from my bottle of rum will help bring me back to normal. Not good for me to have these negative violent thoughts taking over my mind … taking over my day.

Upstairs, I take in my surroundings: a bedroom and bathroom shared with Jose. Safe, protected and loved. I need to focus on that, focus on the good. Chief will take care of the rest. Still, my heart continues to pound in my ears.

I close the bedroom door, then the bathroom door. Hidden behind a stack of white towels, the bottle lies in a cabinet, high above the sink. Sitting on the toilet seat, I sip until the now familiar warmth hits my stomach … the anticipated feeling of relaxation finally taking over my body. Holding the amber bottle up to the light, I note only half the bottle of rum remains. Standing, I carefully hide the bottle away. Again.

On my bed, I close my eyes, returning to my ongoing fantasy of what I'll do to Espinoza when I get five minutes alone with him. My thoughts quickly get out of control—dark, violent, and disturbing. I finally drift off to sleep. I wake with a start, sitting straight up. I was dreaming of vivid, disconnected segments of my childhood mixed with the past year of working for Big Dee. Of the terrified faces of children as I scared them in the darkened Circus Freak Show trailer. Then Poppy drifts through, then runs off when he sees me. What am I doing? I rub my eyes and slump back on the pillow, shame paralyzing me. How had I gotten so far away from being the loving son of a proud Cuban immigrant? Don't tell Mommy. It will break her heart.

My phone vibrates next to me. Picking it up, I read a text from Andy: ON MY WAY OVER. What time is it? 3:30. There was a knock on my bedroom door.

"Come in," I call.

"I just got a call from Chief." Mr. A. comes into the room. "He wants us to come down to the station right away."

16

Smooth Operator

Nearly losing my balance, I stumbled out of bed, willing my feet to find my flip-flops. I need to be operating at 100 percent for this. Wow, drinking before noon! Never a good idea. In the bathroom, I splash cold water onto my face.

"Is this concerning the cold case we were speaking of earlier?" Mr. A. asks, opening the blinds.

I glance out the window. Andy's Jeep is coming up the driveway. Maybe things are popping. "There's Andy. Let's go, sir. Whatever Chief has to say is important. I'll fill you in on the way, okay?" I run ahead of him, down the stairs, starting for the door. Mr. A. follows, snatching his keys from the key rack.

"Okay, I'm all ears." Andy hops in the back as Mr. A. puts the station wagon into gear. "Talk to me."

I describe how Andy and I have come up with the idea of identifying my parents' killer as the cold case project for his final grade. I tell Mr. A. everything, up to the point of finding Mommy's earring this morning.

"I intended to tell you after dinner tonight. I needed to okay it with Chief first." My throat closes, making my voice sound strained. Is he angry because I kept so much from him for so long? I run my fingers through my hair, twisting it behind my ears, realizing too late how much my new father's trust means to me.

"You guys have covered a lot of ground. I wonder what Chief came up with after interrogating that creep." Mr. A. looks excited at the prospect of being included. He speaks quickly, his usually measured words and slow speech gone.

The tension leaves my body. I turn to Andy and laugh. "We watch all the forensic cop shows together. It's our thing." Wow! I have a thing with a parent again. Feels good.

"It's easy to get sucked into the mystery of how evidence and clues can break a case that looks hopeless," Andy says.

"I always look for the human motive behind the crime. It's often greed or revenge," Mr. A. replies as he pulls into the small parking lot at the rear of the stationhouse.

Chief motions us into his office. His face is redder than normal. He sits on the edge of his desk and tugs on his collar. Has something gone terribly wrong? I stare, waiting for him to speak.

"Did Pedro inform you of the cold case?" Mr. A. nods, and Chief continues, "Espinoza came in and answered every one of our questions. He's a smooth operator, that one. It's as if he knew the questions I would ask ahead of time. He had the correct answers ready. Very smug. He was lying through his teeth. I could tell!" Chief bangs his fist hard on the desk.

I jerk upright in my chair. "What did he say?"

"Espinoza said a friend had borrowed the BMW that day and had struck a wall going twenty miles per hour. He claimed no knowledge of the earring or your parents' deaths. His friend returned the car to him, and he got it repaired. He was traveling to Jacksonville the next weekend and had the windshield replaced up there. It was only cracked. So, he could drive the BMW that distance, he claimed."

"So, now what?" Andy asks.

"Until I can prove he was the driver of the BMW, he walks," Chief growls.

"You mean he's out there, as free as you and me?" I bolt from my chair.

"Yep." Chief eyes me. I need to stay cool.

"Did he give you the name of the friend who supposedly was driving his car?" I ask.

"Yes. We have his contact info. I'm running a check on it today. Espinoza said this friend is visiting family in Bogota, Colombia. Convenient, but barely believable." Chief rolls his eyes.

"Did the video incriminate Espinoza?" Andy asks.

"It showed a known crack dealer who met with Espinoza that night. We can't verify what they were doing inside the Crown Vic. Thanks to that video, Andy, we're now aware Espinoza is peddling drugs in Boca. We have sent out a description of every car in the video to all units. We'll keep a close eye on them. Espinoza doesn't suspect we know any of this. He knows we had questions concerning the BMW and looks confident his alibi is airtight. Something about this entire case makes my wrist itch."

"What?" Andy asks. We look on as Chief absently scratches the inside of his left wrist.

"When my left wrist itches, it's my sixth sense informing me I need to go back. I need to comb through every piece of evidence, every document, interview, and case history from the beginning. That I'm missing something in the big picture."

"That would mean going to Hialeah," Mr. A. says.

"Yep. Andy, do you want to join me?" Chief looks at Andy.

"Sure. When do we go?"

"There's no time like right now. Police stations are open 24/7. I'll call down and let them know we're on our way, let them know what we'll require." Chief picks up his phone, holding up the evidence vial with the earring inside. He sticks it in his pocket. I cross my arms, leaning back in my chair. Not included. Left behind.

Andy turns to me. "We'll check in with you as soon as we get back. You realize why you can't go, right?" His tone is muted. I nod, avoiding his eyes.

If this is how "emotionally invested" feels, then yes, I am. One hundred percent. Who cares about busting a couple of drug dealers? This guy needs to be put away for my parents' murder!

Up next, Plan B. The plan I've been hatching to get to Espinoza. In case all else fails.

17

Hanging Out

If Justin stays with his stepdad in Boca on the weekends, then he must hang out somewhere. Boca is a small city with only a few places to hang as far as I've seen. Where to connect with Justin Espinoza? But there has to be another way to get to his stepdad. Doesn't seem like they're very close. Not like Luke and Mr. A.

It's getting dark when Mr. A. and I walk into the silent house. Sara's asleep on the couch while Luke and Danny are sacked out on the floor cushions. Paper plates with crumbs and grease spot circles are scattered across the coffee table. A muted surf video plays on the TV. Mrs. Addison left a note on the counter: Took Jose to the library. Pizzas in the oven.

We sit in the kitchen talking about the case as we finish the last of the pizza. "It looks like they're going to get this Espinoza," Mr. A. says.

"Yeah, but so what? Drug dealers have loads of cash for bail. I need him arrested for murder. Then he can't get out on bail." I can't disguise the bitterness I feel. "You actually have to do the time."

"I don't know how it all works, son. Knowing Chief as I do, he won't let this guy slither through the system until full justice is served." He looks at me. I look away, not used to adults watching my every reaction. It rattles me. But he has to know how I feel.

"That's just it! It's the system I don't trust!" I spit out, staring out the kitchen window into the dark.

"What system?" Sara asks, rubbing the sleep out of her eyes as she joins us. "What's the matter, Pedro?" She drapes her arm around my shoulders, giving me a hug. I glance at Mr. A., wondering what to say.

"We don't keep secrets." He lifts his eyebrows as if asking to continue. I nod, letting out a long breath. It strikes me full force how stressful keeping my secret from these guys has been. "Sara, get Luke and Danny. We have something to tell you." Sara leaves the room. "Do you prefer I tell them or you?"

"You," I whisper, tracing imaginary eights on the countertop. Exhausted, I cross my arms on the counter and lay my head in them.

Luke, Sara, and Danny come into the kitchen. "What's happening?" Luke lays his hand on my shoulder.

"First, I need your promise that what I tell you never leaves this room," Mr. A. says. They all agree. "Andy and Pedro have been working on identifying the individual who drove the car that killed Mr. and Mrs. Ramirez. They've discovered the hit and run car, its owner, and a new damaging piece of evidence. Chief has taken over the case because the primary suspect has moved to Palm Beach County. This person is suspected of selling drugs in the area."

"Wow! When did all this happen?" Danny asks.

"Over the last ten days, with today being the big day as far as getting a break in the case," Mr. A. says. "Pedro is concerned the police will book this guy on drug charges, that he'll make bail and run ... never convicted of the Ramirezes' murders."

"Now I see why you're so upset." Sara rubs my shoulder. Not raising my head, I nod. "I don't blame you. You constantly hear of people going free on a technicality when they're guilty as sin."

Danny asks, "So, what happens now?"

"Chief and Andy have gone to the Hialeah Police Station to sift through their cold case evidence bin. They should be back later tonight." Looking up, I stare out the window again.

"Hey Pedro, we were going downtown to catch a movie. Why don't you come, too? It'll get your mind off things until they get back," Sara says.

"Yeah," Luke adds. "I need a new leash for my surfboard while we're there. The one I had snapped in the water today. Gigantic waves."

I smile. "I appreciate what you're doing, guys. Thanks. Yeah, let's go."

"Pedro, I need you to act like a sixteen-year-old and have fun. By the way, guys, Jose doesn't know about any of this. We'll tell him when you think the time is right, Pedro," Mr. A. says. "Before you go, let's say a prayer." We hold one another's hands while Mr. A. leads. "Jesus, You've brought these two precious souls into our home, and we thank You from the bottom of our hearts. Please lead us to a safe and speedy resolution to the source of pain in Pedro and Jose's hearts, the senseless and brutal death of their beloved parents. Help us support them in Your loving way. In Jesus's name. Amen."

In Danny's car, we talk about the case. "Chief cut through the red tape fast. Right now, he and Andy are in Hialeah getting things done. It would've taken at least two more weeks if the original deadbeat detective had his way. I don't understand. He did a half-job the first time. How could he ask that the inquiry be postponed until he came back from his vacation?"

"If anybody can cut through the bunk, Chief can," Luke says. "He's an old-fashioned kind of investigator. With him, you have your own private detective."

"Yeah, I got that impression, too. My biggest fear is they'll go after Espinoza as a crack dealer, not a murderer. Then he won't get what's really coming to him. I can't help it. I want Espinoza to do his time for the actual crime!" They look surprised at the passion in my voice.

"But he's both those things, bro. If they get him on drugs, then at least they'll have him captive until they can prove the murder. Chief won't let you down," Luke says.

"I hope not. My brother and I have been let down by both the police and the social service system before. Who knows where we'd be if your family hadn't taken us in?" I shiver. "Sleeping on the cold, hard ground in a torn sleeping bag someplace far north of here."

We walk along the sidewalk of Tansy Park. I take my phone out and look at the picture of Justin Espinoza one more time. Danny sees it and asks who it is. Hesitating, I tell him, passing my phone around. "I took it last night at the swim meet. I felt bad for the dude. He's scoring points for his team, and his dad's out in front of our school selling crack."

"That's the lowest," Sara says.

"Yeah, but there's more. His parents are in the middle of a divorce. They have a nice house in Hialeah, where his mom lives, but it's for sale. He has to come up here on weekends and stay with Espinoza."

"I wonder what he's like. Wow! Check out at that unibrow." Sara smiles, handing the phone back.

"It's clearly a distinguishing feature. And I wonder how long his hair is under that swim cap," Danny says.

"Anyone's guess," I answer. We arrive at the ticket window. Choosing the surf movie, we continue into the darkened theater. I watch as Sara curls up next to Danny. From our conversation at church Wednesday night, I get the impression it scared Danny to get close to her. As if she'd reject him. It didn't look that way now, here in the dark. Maybe Danny is still wary of how Luke will react. I hope for the best for these two. Real-life connections can slip away in an instant. The pang in my stomach hits me fresh. I miss my parents so much.

After the movie, Sara announces, "I need chocolate ice cream. Let's head over to the ice cream parlor. I'm buying." We sit on the steps around the fountain, eating ice cream, watching the crowds walk by. Then I see him. I nudge Luke, pointing to a dude our age. He's sitting alone on a bench across the court, skateboard propped up on his knee. He has black, wavy, shoulder-length hair and an unmistakable unibrow. Danny spots Justin next. We stand up.

"What?" Sara asks, biting into her chocolate cone. "Oh!" She spots him and stands up too. "Doesn't look as if he has any friends!" Justin catches us staring at him. "Busted." Sara grins, waving him over.

18

Justin

"What are you doing?" Luke hisses at his sister.

"It looks like he could use a friend or two tonight. That's all. I mean it's not as if we don't know his story," she says.

"Yeah, well, let's not tell him that," I mutter under my breath as Justin rolls up on his skateboard, flipping it up with his toe, braking in front of us.

"Hey, dude, do you swim for Callahan?" Luke asks.

"Sure do."

"We're on the Boca team. I recognize you from the meet last night. This is my sister Sara, Pedro, and Danny."

"Hey! Good to meet you guys. Name's Justin. Yeah, your team beat us up pretty bad last night. We'll get you next time." He laughs.

"You're a long way from home," Danny says.

"Yeah, long story," Justin says. "So, what are you guys up to tonight?"

"We were about to head over to the surf shop," Luke says. "Do you surf?"

"Since before I could stand up!" Justin grins. "My uncle taught me when I was three. We'd go out, two on a board, plus his dog."

"He must be pretty good," Danny says.

"He's a pro on the circuit. All the endorsements and stuff. Dennis Dean. Ever heard of him?"

"Denny Dean? Who hasn't?" Luke exclaims. "Do you have your board here? We caught some decent waves this morning. Tomorrow's looking even better."

"No. It's home in Hialeah. Collecting dust. Haven't surfed in a while." Justin looks down, his smile fading. We start toward the surf store, talking along the way. From the way he talks, Justin sounds like he's a skilled surfer. He surfed Hawaii and Cali. We shop for Luke's new leash, buy some wax and a few decals, then wander back up the boardwalk, checking out the store windows. One store's putting up Christmas decorations already.

"It won't seem like Christmas at our house this year," Justin says. "My parents are going through a divorce. Things are tense."

"That's got to be tough," Danny says.

"Yeah. They're fighting over me. My mom married this guy, Craig, when I was twelve, and he adopted me. That was four years ago. Now that they're getting a divorce, he claims he has a legitimate right to me. He drags me up here on the weekends, away from my mom and friends, as if I'm his real kid. I sit around and play computer games all weekend while my friends back home are out surfing the waves at South Beach. Lawyers are fighting over my custody. My mom says there isn't anything she can do about it for now."

"Wow! Do you know where your real dad is?" I ask.

"No. He lives someplace in Cuba or Costa Rica. Uncle Denny is his brother. Says someday he'll take me to meet him. In the meantime, my mom forbids it. Pretty messed up all around."

"Sounds it." I nod. Thank you, Lord, for the Addisons, who love Jose and me with no strings attached.

"It's not as if my stepdad cares much about me. Most of the time he's sleeping—or away. He bought a nice condo on the ocean, but there's no furniture in it. We sleep on those blow-up mattresses. Our house in Hialeah is my real home."

"Here's my car." Danny stops at the curb. "I'm ready to head home, get some sleep, and hit the waves in the AM. Do you need a ride, dude?"

"No, that's my stepdad cruising down the street in that black car." He waves Craig Espinoza down. My heart thumps wildly. As the car pulls up, the dark tinted driver's window opens. Suddenly, we're face to face with Espinoza. I step behind Luke on the slim chance Espinoza might recognize me.

"Get in, kid. I'm running late," Espinoza orders Justin in a harsh tone while holding his cell to his ear.

"See you around. I guess." Justin walks to the other side of the car.

"Yeah," Luke says. "Hey, we surf Deerfield Beach, north side of the pier, if you can make it tomorrow morning. You can use my board. Help me break in my new leash."

"Cool! Thanks." Justin sounds doubtful at the prospect but smiles, looking glad to be invited. The car speeds off.

I'm shaking from head to toe. "What just happened?" I ask no one in particular. Did Plan B just fall into my lap?

"What just happened is someone who needed some friends just found them. Now he knows where to meet up again," Sara states.

"He doesn't seem too attached to his stepdad, does he?" Danny asks.

"Not really. We only know a bit of the story though. I wonder if he'll show up to surf in the morning," Luke says.

"I'll be there in case he does. He's not at all what I thought. I expected a tough, Miami street type ... not a regular dude who surfs," I say.

"We'll have to wait till tomorrow to know him better. If he shows. Let's go. Chief and Andy may be back from Hialeah." Sara pulls out her phone, reading the time.

"Ten-thirty." Danny looks over at her. "Don't worry. I'm watching out for your curfew." He puts the car in gear and pulls onto the road. We make it home just in time.

19

Bad News

Danny drops us off with the promise to return in six hours. Mr. and Mrs. Addison are waiting in the kitchen. Jose is already in bed.

Waiting for everyone else to get in, I sit at the counter, stand up, then sit down again, running my fingers through my hair. What's taking so long? Sara saying good night to Danny of course! Everyone finally pulls their stools up to the counter.

"What happened in Hialeah?" I look at Mr. A. His face is neutral. What's he holding back?

"Andy just left. He and Chief returned with bad news." He turns to me. "Today was a productive one—mostly. You found the car, your mother's earring, and Espinoza's address. The bad news is the original evidence box has disappeared."

"What?" I jump up. My stool crashes to the floor. "How can that be?" I stoop to pick it up. With the palm of my hand, I tap the back of the stool, making it slowly spin full circle. I can't sit, needing to do something.

"When Chief and Andy arrived at the station in Hialeah, their Chief of Police was waiting. He explained he couldn't locate the box of physical evidence Chief Howell was seeking. It was checked out of the cold case repository two weeks ago by a Detective Andecker and never returned. This is the same detective who is on vacation in Colombia."

"Yeah, the same jerk who requested that we wait until he returns before proceeding with Mommy and Poppy's investigation." My jaw's tight. "What's that guy afraid of?"

"That's precisely what Chief Howell wants to know," Mr. A. says.

"Does this Detective Andecker have an office they can search?" I ask.

"He said they had searched Andecker's office and turned up nothing."

"Can't they search his house?" I slap the stool back hard, making it spin around as fast as it will go.

"You'll have to wait till tomorrow to ask Chief. I'm so sorry, Pedro." He puts his arm around my shoulders and stops the spinning stool with his other hand. "This may only be a slight setback. The evidence could turn up tomorrow."

My shoulders slump, energy draining out of me. "Yeah ... you're probably right. Do you mind if I hop online and chat with Andy?" What does Andy think the next step will be?

"No problem. I'm heading to bed," Mrs. Addison declares.

"That makes two of us. It's been a long day. Sara, will you lock up before turning in?" Mr. A. pats me on the back before heading to his bedroom.

"Sure, Dad. We're going to watch TV, keep Pedro company." Sara follows Luke and me into the den. "Maybe Andy has something to add."

I shake my head, sighing while logging onto the computer. "We need to learn more about this Detective Andecker. He's starting to stink like a three-day-old fish, too. Let's hear Andy's take on all this." I message Andy. Luke and Sara crowd around the screen.

Me: Dude, you there?

Andy: Waiting for you. Did your dad tell you the latest?

Me: Yeah. What do you think?

Andy: It stinks. I don't know what to think.

Me: Should we do a background check on Andecker?

Andy: Personal or professional?

I look up at Luke. "I'd say personal. Where he lives, who his family is, that info. We don't even have his first name," Luke says.

Me: Personal. Full name, address, family, stuff like that.

Andy: That usually costs money, but I may be able to get it through the university server. If I get blocked because he's in law enforcement,

I'll scroll social media and hope for the best. I still have that photo you sent me.

Me: That would be great. I have a bad feeling about this guy. Nothing he does is right.

Andy: Yeah, so does Chief. He was outraged. Barely spoke on the way home. Scratched his wrist constantly.

"Should we tell Andy about meeting Justin?" Luke asks.

"Let's not muddle matters with that right now," Sara says. I nod, but for my own reasons.

Andy: I'm driving back to Miami early tomorrow morning. I'll be in touch if I find anything.

Me: Be safe. FYI, my dad told Luke, Sara, Danny.

Andy: Cool. You guys coming down for the game Saturday? We can check out any addresses we come up with for Andecker.

Me: For sure.

Andy: Later

Me: Later

"Andy is a good friend," I say, getting up to let Luke use the computer. I need a walk and a cigarette. Then a sip of rum to get to sleep.

"Wait. Luke. Show Pedro that Bible website, Bible Gateway. You spend enough time online that you should know where to go to read the Bible, Pedro." Luke brings up the site and shows me how to get around in it. "There are lots of Bible versions, but I keep it set to *The Message*. It's kinda bold and in your face with how it translates verses. I think you'll like it."

Luke reads, "'*God is good, a hiding place in tough times. He recognizes and welcomes anyone looking for help, no matter how desperate the trouble is.*' He's inviting anyone who is desperate, to seek Him, Pedro."

"Gotcha. Thanks, you guys. I'll check it out. Think I'll go for a walk before going to bed. I won't forget to lock up when I come in. Good night." I finger the cigarette lighter in my pocket. I wish getting rid of this revengeful feeling with a verse from the Bible was that simple. Yet, they seem to know it to be true. But they never suffered the loss of both parents, then came face to face with their killer. Words on a computer screen for comfort? No, I don't think so. Inhaling deeply from my cigarette, the calm seeps over me.

When I return, the house is dark and quiet. Jose is fast asleep, a peaceful look on his face. I slip into the bathroom and take a long drink from my bottle of rum. Three quarters empty. I need to slow down to make the rum last. Wide awake, I creep downstairs and sit in the dark den. Finishing the night off with a victorious kill game will help me fall asleep.

20

Sunday Surfing

Tap, tap, pause, tap. I hear Danny's early morning surf knock. My phone reads 6:00 AM. Ugh! Didn't I just close my eyes? From the top of the stairs, I watch Sara dash through the quiet house to let Danny in.

"Good morning, beautiful," Danny says as she opens the door.

"Hi." Danny leans in and whispers something in her ear, then catches sight of me coming down the stairs.

"Don't let me interrupt." I smile, continuing to the kitchen, nodding to Luke, who's sitting at the counter. They follow me. Sara begins packing food for the day. She stacks containers of watermelon and sliced fruit, granola bars, and a carton of orange juice into an old beat-up basket.

"Where did you get that old picnic basket?" Danny laughs.

"A garage sale. Don't disrespect my basket, or you'll get nothing out of it when your stomach growls," Sara warns.

"I was going to offer to fix it up for you." Danny smiles. "Give it a coat of shellac, tighten a few screws, add a little TLC, and it'll be like new."

"That will get you a month's worth of treats." Sara beams at Danny.

"Deal."

Luke pulls towels out of the dryer from the day before. They're still wet. "Oh no! I put them in and forgot to turn the dryer on. Now what?"

"That's what you get when you text and dry." Sara laughs. "Maybe Cheree will have an extra?"

"I have dry ones in my bathroom," I offer. Luke and Sara stare at me in horror.

"He doesn't know," Luke says in a dramatic tone.

"We should tell him." Sara's serious. "Now."

"What?" I glance at Danny, who looks as puzzled as I am.

"You never, never take one of Mom's bathroom towels out the front door," Luke says.

"She'll change the locks and you won't get back in. Ever!" Sara is trying to be dramatic but ends up giggling. I'm relieved but confused. "That was Mom's last threat after Luke and I swiped one too many towels for the pool or beach. I guess she prefers her bathroom towels to match or something. You can use mine, Luke. I'm not going in the water. Too cold."

A cold front blew through during the night. It's windy and cool. When we get to the beach, Sara and I sit on the deck of Kelly's Diner, a small restaurant on the boardwalk. Luke and Danny catch wave after wave.

***

"Hi Sara." I look up to see a girl with short blonde hair standing next to our table. She's wearing a Boca South sweatshirt. I've never seen her at school. Sara gets up to give her a hug.

"Piper! How are you? Sit with us. This is my brother, Pedro. Pedro, Piper. Piper is a new friend from school. My only new friend from school." She laughs. I stand up, giving Piper my seat. "What are you up to?"

"Nothing much." Piper sounds down. "I woke up this morning, and our apartment was cold and empty. My mom was gone. There was no food in the refrigerator. I came to Kelly's for hot chocolate. What brings you guys here?"

"Luke and Danny are surfing. We're just trying to stay warm," Sara says. "I think fall is definitely here." Just then, the long black Crown Vic glides up. I freeze, then step behind the post I was leaning on. I can see him, but he can't see me. Espinoza is so close... The skin on my neck and chest feels like a thousand little pin pricks just hit. Justin gets out, then reaches inside for his backpack. He nods to Espinoza, closes the door, and the car speeds away. I take a deep breath. Relax. Chill.

"Who's that?" Piper asks. "I haven't seen him around."

"Then I'll introduce you. Justin!" Sara calls. Justin glances around, spots us, and waves. He walks over as Sara gets up to greet him. "Hey, Justin. This is my friend Piper."

"Nice to meet you, Piper. Wow! Check out those waves." Justin stares out at the ocean.

"Hey, Justin, glad you could make it. Here, grab my board. I'm new to surfing and don't have the endurance those guys have," I offer.

"I'll take care of your backpack. The water looks a wee bit chilly." Sara shivers.

"Thanks!" In a single motion, Justin drops his backpack, picks up my board, and takes off toward the water.

"Wow! Like I said, Sara. Who is that? He's hot," Piper says.

"He's a kid on the Callahan High swim team. Lives up here on the weekends with his dad. We recognized him from Friday's swim meet when we were hanging out at Tansy Park last night. He hung with us for a while. The guys invited him to surf with them this morning," Sara says.

Justin plunges into the water and paddles out past the break. The guys wave him over. After catching a few more good waves, Danny surfs onto the shore. He steps onto Kelly's patio, shivering in the cool October air. Sara digs his towel out of his bag and drapes it around him. He catches her in a quick hug and says, "The towel isn't enough! I require body heat!"

"Do you want some hot chocolate? This place sells it by the carafe!" Sara pours Danny a mug, then opens the lid of her basket for the rest of us to help ourselves.

"I'm in. Hi, Piper." Danny smiles, warming his hands on the mug. "The air is getting colder. We should go inside."

"I want to check out Justin surfing. He sounded super into it last night." Sara scans the water.

"He's looking good, from what I've seen so far," I say. "Lots of fancy moves."

"Yeah. Too bad he got here so late. It's flattening out. Another half hour of surfing and the waves will be gone," Danny replies. "Wow! Did you see that? He's got some great moves! Watch! I'll bet you Luke's going to try to do the same thing." Danny howls. "I shouldn't laugh. Imitation is how you become a better surfer."

"Watch Luke try what?" Cheree asks, strolling onto the patio wearing the latest in surf fashion.

"Hey Cheree! Over here. No work today? Yay!" Sara says.

"No! Thank goodness. I needed a break from those tire-kicking customers," Cheree exclaims.

"If it weren't for those tire-kicking customers, you wouldn't be driving around in that pretty white Mustang," Danny teases.

"Yeah, well, so what about all that? At least I know how to put in a twelve-hour day when necessary!" Cheree replies, crooking her arm and showing us her muscle. "As long as it isn't often. Like once a year. Is that Luke in the black board shorts? Who's the other guy?"

"Yeah, Luke is in black. The other guy, Justin from Miami, is on Pedro's board. We were downtown last night and recognized him from the swim meet on Friday. He said he surfed. So, we asked him to come this morning. He's good, too. His uncle is Denny Dean." Sara pours Cheree a hot chocolate.

"Denny Dean! I'd give money to meet him. He's one of the all-time greats!" Cheree digs into her bag and pulls out a surf magazine, holding it out so we can see. The cover photo features a crouching surfer riding the inside of a glassy barrel wave. "Look, he's on the cover of *Surf It! Magazine.*" Danny takes the magazine and begins paging through it.

"Hi, I'm Cheree," she says to Piper.

"Piper Clark. You don't go to Boca South, do you?"

"No, I go to the performing arts school in West Palm. I live in Boca though."

"Piper's my new friend from school." Sara looks up. "Hey, here come the guys. Cheree, do you have an extra towel? Luke forgot to dry his." She points to Luke and Justin getting out of the water. Cheree takes a pink towel from her bag and runs toward Luke, hair and towel blowing in the wind. A big grin spreads across Luke's face.

"Looking good out there, Justin," Danny calls as they come up the steps. Justin smiles his thanks.

"All that surfing made me hungry." Luke rubs his stomach. "We should go to The Grand Slam Palace." Agreed! It's time for hot food.

21

Four Friends

"I'll need a ride," Justin says. "Could someone drop me off at the Tri-Rail Station after breakfast? I hate to impose, but it was hard to say no to your offer last night. Otherwise, I'd just be hanging out with my stepdad. He's either on the phone or stomping around, angry at the person he was talking to."

"You can come surf with us anytime," Luke says. "I got lots of good tips today while checking out your moves."

"I can take you to the train," Piper offers. "I live near the station."

"Okay. Let's meet at the Grand Slam and pig out." Sara gathers her things. Danny picks up her picnic basket. I catch his eye and smirk. He's working it hard.

We crowd into the largest circular booth at the restaurant. I make sure to sit next to Justin. Since we met, it's tough to regard him as a means for getting close to his creep of a stepfather. Where Luke and Danny have an easygoing vibe with him, I'm stiff and awkward when I try to join in. So, I don't. The guilt of using him for my purposes bugs me. We'd probably be friends under any other circumstances. What does he think of me?

The guys are riding on their surfing high, everybody in a good mood. Cheree brings the magazine with Justin's uncle out. We pour over the pictures of Denny Dean surfing at different beaches, famous beaches I'd like to go to someday.

"You're so lucky to have him as your uncle," I say. Did someone just ask that? I'm not sure. Awkward.

He looks over at me. "Gracias." So, he acknowledges our shared Latino culture. That's a start. I glance at him, then look away.

"Tonight, Danny, Pedro, and I are speaking with our youth pastor, Jonas. We want to organize a Spring Break Surf/Bible Camp in Costa Rica. Have you been there, Justin?" Luke asks.

"No, but I'd be stoked to go. I don't know much about the Bible. My mom's Catholic, but my dad never took us to church," Justin says.

"No worries. I'm using Bible training wheels, too." I laugh. "The Bible is a big book." Stay on common ground and things will go well. But remember the big picture. Always.

"Spring is a long time away." Justin looks down at the table, drawing circles with his forefinger. "Lots happening at home these days."

"It'll all work itself out, I'm sure," Sara says. Ha! I know better. More trouble is headed Justin's way, with a stepdad who's a murderer and a crack dealer.

"Besides, you have friends in Palm Beach County, where the waves are good!" Luke says. "Bring your board up next weekend for sure."

"My stepdad is spending next weekend in Miami. So, I'll have to see. I should get going. It takes two hours to get to Miami. The trains stop running early on Sundays." Justin looks at Piper. She smiles up at him, slinging her backpack over her shoulder.

"Here, call yourself so we'll have each other's cell numbers." I pass my phone to Justin. "Text us if you get into town next weekend. We'll be at the beach both mornings if there's surf." Luke and Danny hand him their phones, too.

"Cool!" Justin gets up and says goodbye, leaving with a smiling Piper in tow. Great! Things are developing nicely. Plan B is moving along. I look up to see Danny, Luke, and Sara watching me. I shake my head slightly, hoping they won't say anything.

"Okay, what's going on here?" Cheree demands. "Is Justin Espinoza the son of that creep who turned that BMW in last week? The clunker, which I might add, has been impounded as a murder weapon?" She stares at each of us. Luke looks at me, lifting his eyebrows. I nod, giving him permission to tell Cheree. She already knows half the story.

After swearing her to secrecy, Luke tells her what we know so far. "Yes, Justin is the son of the dude with the BMW, Craig Espinoza. His team from Callahan swam against us on Friday. Pedro took a picture of him. We recognized him when we were at Tansy Park last night, and Sara invited him to join us today. He's a chill dude living in the middle of some bad news. He doesn't know that we're aware his dad is a murder suspect. The police in Hialeah lost all the evidence in the case."

"What evidence?" Cheree looks baffled.

"Again, you can't tell anyone, Cheree, not even your dad," I repeat. "That BMW is the car that was used to kill my parents in a hit and run over a year and a half ago. In Hialeah. We found my mom's earring in the windshield wiper drain grill. The other earring is in the original evidence box in Hialeah. Somehow, the police lost the evidence box within the past ten days."

"Wow! This is super serious stuff," Cheree says.

"Super serious. And secret." I met her eyes.

"That's not all," Luke continues. "Now we find out Justin's parents are divorcing. His stepdad, Craig Espinoza, is living in Boca and suspected of peddling crack."

"Craig, the BMW dude, right? This is getting complicated," Cheree says.

"Right. I'm just afraid Espinoza will slip away before we can pin the murders on him. It's as if everybody involved is taking a trip to Bogota, Columbia, these days." As I say these words out loud, we all look around at each other. I lean back, my body going perfectly still. Did those guys just reach the same conclusion? "How did we not see this before? They are probably moving drugs into Miami. Justin said his stepdad was staying in Miami next weekend." My thoughts swirling, I connect the dots that lead to this scenario.

I stare out the window. This is huge. Are we overreacting, or is this the truth? Did Chief suspect and not bring us into the loop? Who can I trust? Too much is happening too fast. I pick up the salt and pepper shakers and start tapping them together, struggling to figure things out. My mind blanks out ... my thoughts frozen inside.

Just then, my phone vibrates on the table. I look down and read the text from Andy out loud: DETECTIVE ANDECKER IS ESPINOZA'S BROTHER-IN-LAW. LIVES ON THE SAME STREET IN HIALEAH. 122ND.

"So, that's why the evidence box disappeared, why there was no investigation into my parents' death." I tap the saltshaker on the table more forcefully with each word. My ears pound. "Andecker has the authority of the law behind him. He's the detective! He'll never get caught because he can stay one step ahead. Always!"

I throw the pepper shaker into the booth across the aisle and bolt for the door. Luke and Danny follow me out to the sidewalk, where I run up the street. Stopping at the corner, I fold my arms across my chest, struggling to calm myself, needing to puke. My wonderful parents were innocent victims, dead because they were drawn into a large drug cartel by pure chance. Yeah, a dirty cop can cause all kinds of evidence to disappear. Poof! I bend over and throw up my breakfast into the gutter.

Luke puts his hand on my shoulder. "Hey! Easy, Pedro. Let's talk this through. You don't know Chief Howell. He's like a dog with a bone when things don't make sense. He'll sort this out. I'm certain of it." Luke is doing his best to reassure me, but his words aren't erasing the bitter taste in my mouth, the hot tears stinging the back of my eyes.

Danny says, "Andy wants to solve this for you more than ever, Pedro. We were talking last night about ways we can support you as you go through this. Go slow. Give it a few days." Listening to my friends' words, I know they're doing what friends do, talking me off the ledge. I take a deep breath and let my arms flop to my sides. Yes, they're speaking the truth I need to hear.

These guys care. It feels solid. I haven't had this feeling in a long time. Too long. Is this what Jose has been experiencing with Mr. and Mrs. Addison? They're right. It has only been two days since things broke in the case. The tension leaves my body. All I want to do is take a nap. This case has been consuming me since I saw Espinoza at the swim meet.

"Thanks, guys. It's so painful. I can't sleep... It's all I think of." We turn and walk back to the car, where Sara and Cheree are waiting. Sara puts her arms around me. One by one, they join in a group hug.

As she does at the strangest times, Sara's bows her head and boldly prays: "Father, thank you for Your revelations in this case. We're praying for our brother Pedro, who is so hurt by the senseless deaths of his mom and dad. We can't know the pain he carries 24/7. You are an able God. Able to do anything. Please give Pedro Your peace as he goes through this ordeal. In Jesus's name. Amen."

"Thanks, Sara. And you guys, too. Hey, do you think I'll have time for a nap before church tonight?"

22

Divine Appointment

I'm struggling to keep my mind on the sermon. Sure, things might go smoother for me if I listened, then worked to apply the teachings of the Bible. But tonight, my thoughts are much louder than Pastor Thomas's words. My mind races again, turning over all the new facts we learned since the swim meet. Excusing myself, I slip out the front door into the cool evening air.

The heat from the long, hot summer has finally broken. Change is in the air. Fall used to be my favorite season. I take a deep breath. Life used to be simple ... should still be. School, kicking an old soccer ball around the street, family dinners, school art projects. But it isn't. Not for me. Not now. Now these daily activities are distracting, keeping me from running after what I know I need to do. What I promised myself. For Mommy and Poppy.

Stomach churning, I kick the tire of a red truck as I walk by. Ow! That didn't help. It only makes me madder. They murdered my parents because two drug traffickers thought my dad saw too much. I'm sure Andecker was in on that drug deal. He needed to make sure my parents' death wasn't investigated to protect himself and Espinoza. He probably arranged the hit and run. He had too much to lose. A dirty cop, for sure. I want to rip them both apart limb from limb.

I gaze up at the steeple and a short, dry laugh escapes my lips. These violent, vengeful thoughts don't belong inside a church—or even a church parking lot. I need to know if there's a drug deal in the works in Miami this weekend, only five days away. Chief Howell would be the one to talk to. Andy, too. I pull out my phone.

"Hey, what's going on?" I ask him.

"Still trying to fit all the parts of this puzzle together."

"Super simple to me. They were both in on it, the crack house and the double murder of my parents." My words come across bitter. I work to control my emotions.

"Yeah. Problem is... What's next? Who are they working for? We don't want to tip anybody off. Then they'll all run back to Colombia like the cockroaches they are. Have you spoken with Chief?"

"Not yet. I'm still at church. We should be home by 8:00."

"In the end, we have to follow Chief's lead. He's in charge. I feel for you, Pedro. I really do. Have you visited your parents' graves lately?"

"No. Never. The social services people gave me the name of a cemetery in West Dade County. We've never been there. What does it matter? They're dead and gone." I can't shake my bitterness.

"It might help if you went. To say goodbye."

"Yeah, maybe. That's the part that hurts the most. I never got to say goodbye."

"I can take you guys. Text me the name of the cemetery when you get a chance. I'll look it up. We can ride out there one day soon. In the meantime, try to take it easy. We'll get this straightened out."

"Okay, thanks." People are coming out of the church. I shuffle over to Danny's car, my shoulders sagging. What's the use of chasing the past? Is it worth the agony? It was easier to block out thoughts of our tragedy when I didn't have to talk about it ... deal with people's questions ... consider their suggestions. Andy's just trying to be helpful. Shaking my head, I try to make the confusion go away. Tonight, I'll finish what's left of my rum. That'll help.

Hearing a rustling to my left, I glance over. Jonas is hauling a heavy box out to his car. "Need a hand?"

"Yeah, sure. If you could just open the tailgate." After sliding the box into the back, he turns and smiles. "What are you doing out here by yourself?"

I shrug. "Couldn't focus. I have a lot going on in my life these days."

"Anything you need to talk about?"

"I'm not able to talk about it. Legal matters, I guess you'd call them." Noting his slight frown, I laugh. "I'm not in trouble or anything like that. But yeah, you might be able to help me with something."

Jonas sits on the tailgate, motioning me to do the same, waiting for me to speak. "After my parents' death, the social service system and then touring with the circus took all my time and energy. I was in survival mode, looking out for Jose. I didn't give much thought to visiting my parents' graves. Now I'm feeling kinda guilty but still don't want to go. I don't know why." Swallowing hard, I turn away, watching cars leave the lot.

After a minute, Jonas asks, "Is there anyone you'd want to go with?"

"Well, Jose, of course. The Addison family? I don't know... Andy, Danny's brother, offered to take us. But everybody is so busy. I don't think I could ask them to take a day trip down to West Dade. I don't even know where the cemetery is. Or where their graves are. I don't know..." I trail off. "And then what? Stand around and stare at a piece of grass?"

"Hmm! A visit to a gravesite is different for everyone. There's nothing saying you're obligated to go just yet. You can go anytime."

"Yeah, but then there's Jose. What if he needs to go?" Torn, I look toward the church entrance and see my brother. Have I neglected his needs in my quest for vengeance? Why did Andy have to bring up the cemetery tonight? I need to stay focused.

"Why don't you get Jose and meet me in my office? We can talk about it together and come up with a plan that works for both of you. I don't want to send you home when you're in such distress, Pedro. I'll find Luke and Sara and tell them I'll give you guys a ride." Running my fingers through my hair, I leave to get Jose.

When Jonas comes back to his office, we're there waiting. Jose's poring through the flyers from Costa Rica that were spread across Jonas's desk. "Hey, Jose, do you surf?" Jonas asks.

"No way. There are sharks out there! Big ones. When I get to be a stronger swimmer, I'll surf. Luke is giving me swimming lessons. Hey, why are we here?" He looks at me, then back at Jonas.

"Pedro and I were talking about your parents, how he's sad that they're gone," Jonas begins.

"Yeah. I get sad at the same time every night, just before I fall asleep. I miss them so much. Sometimes I think they'll walk right into our room. Like they did every night when they were alive." Jose looks down, his voice falling to just a whisper.

"Do you remember the night the police told us Mommy and Poppy were gone?"

"A little. The last time I saw them was that morning, eating breakfast. Who knew I'd never hug them again?" Tears roll down his cheeks as he looks at Jonas. He rubs them aside. I move my chair closer and put my arm around him.

After a few moments, Jonas says, "When people we love die, we have a funeral or memorial for them. Next, we take them to a cemetery and bury them in graves. That's one way we can say goodbye until we see them again in heaven."

"We didn't do any of that," I say. "They whisked us off to a large holding facility for displaced juveniles. Locked up, like we were criminals or something. A few days later, a lady brought us a box with a few of my parents' things. Jewelry and stuff from my mother's purse. We never learned what happened to our home or anything."

"Like my baseball card collection and my cool ninja bed sheets. Who has them now?" Jose demands. "And where are my parents buried? We just have the name of a place somewhere in Miami." In the safety of Jonas's office, we let out our grief and sadness. The heartache of the previous eighteen months washes over me like waves in the ocean. Jose and I hold on to each other, heaving with sobs. After a while, Jonas gets up, saying he'll be back with sodas.

"I think we need to go see our parents' graves," I say when he returns. Jose nods.

"Whenever you're ready, guys. It doesn't have to be right away."

"Do you think Mr. and Mrs. Addison will be hurt if we want to visit our real parents?" Jose asks.

"No way," Jonas reassures him. "They might even have ideas to offer for a memorial. You need to talk to them. Let them hear your feelings, your thoughts. I'd be honored to help. But before we go, let's pray." He gathers us in a circle and bow our heads, "Father in heaven, thank You for bringing Pedro to me in his time of great need. Thank You for the healing that has begun in these boys' hearts and lives. Please direct our steps to bring these young souls to full restoration from the aches and pains life has inflicted upon them. In Jesus's name. Amen."

"Did you know I was out in the parking lot?" I ask as we walk to Jonas's truck.

"No, but God did. That's called a 'divine appointment.' In His perfect time, He sends us to help each other. We just don't realize it."

Jose's mouth falls open as he takes a step back. "Wow, cool!" I laugh at his reaction, watching him catch the concept of divine appointments.

"Yes, He works in and through us. Now I need to get you two home so we can let the Addison's in on what we've been talking about."

23

Amazing Grace

We walk in the front door, my arm around Jose's shoulders. Pulling my hood off, I say, "Who loves this perfect weather? The heat has finally broken, the endless summer over. Fall is my favorite season!"

"Hey, what's up?" Luke does a double take. Yeah, I don't say much, I guess. That was a long speech for me. Laughing, I high-five him for emphasis.

"We need to get you guys together to talk something out," Jonas says. Luke leads us to the kitchen, where Mr. and Mrs. Addison are sitting. Sara walks in, still Facetiming with Danny. They say a quick good night.

"Hi, Jonas. Thanks for bringing my guys home," Mrs. Addison says. "You look so serious. Is everything okay?" We sit on the stools around the kitchen island.

Jonas looks at me. I say, "Jose and I have been on the run for so long with the circus ... existing as best we could. We had no time to look back. No time to visit our parents' graves."

"Yeah! And we were talking about it with Jonas. We want to go," Jose says.

"I explained to the guys that under normal circumstances, there'd be a funeral or memorial followed by a burial. That never took place. The foster care folks handed them their parents' death certificates along with the name of the cemetery where they were buried. There's been no closure for these two, physically, mentally, or emotionally."

"Then we'll change that." Mrs. Addison comes over, putting her arms around our shoulders. "Do you have any ideas about how you want to handle the memorial? We'll do whatever you come up with." She looks back and forth at us. I shake my head and swallow, not knowing how to answer. What is a proper request? They are our family now. They want to do this for us. For Mommy and Poppy.

I look over at Jose, who has gone silent.

"How about you two agree on when you'd like to honor your parents' memory. We'll take the day off from work and school. After a special service and lunch, we'll drive down to the cemetery. How does that sound?"

I nod. Still, the words won't come. We've somehow landed in the home of the kindest people on the planet. That they'd do all this for Jose and me...

"In the meantime, may we see any photos you have of your parents? We can scan them and make a slideshow. Would you like that?" Mr. A. gets up, clearing the island of his newspaper.

Nodding, I leave to get the packet of photos I've been carrying around for so long. I spread them on the counter in the order they were taken. Jose's face lights up. Soon, the stories behind the family pictures come pouring out. Jonas scribbles notes on the back of an envelope. Our memorial is taking shape.

Luke taps a photo of Jose and me with Poppy wearing our red and white baseball uniforms, holding up a tall trophy. "Did you guys play senior league?"

"Oh, yeah!" Jose grabs the picture. "Because of our ages, my dad coached both our teams. Poppy was in the minor league in Cuba. He taught us strategies the other teams didn't know, calling it 'the finer points.' He loved baseball."

"That was the year our team won the title. We traveled with the All Stars. Every Thursday night we'd clean out Poppy's work van. That is, if we had an overnight game upstate. Mommy packed it up, and we'd leave on Friday to find a campground. The rest of the team traveled with us. Jose and I pitched our ten-man tent once we got there. Mommy and Poppy slept on a blow-up mattress inside the van."

"What fun!" Sara picks up a photo of us sitting at a picnic table eating arepas cubanas. Jose was mugging the camera.

"It was. Mommy was great at making meals on a camp grill." Jose gently touches the photo where her face is, then looks up. "We had the biggest bonfires in the campground! Other people hung out by our fire because it was so tall. Poppy had a special way of piling the logs. He called it his 'chimenea.' He said he'd teach us how to make one, one day." He peers out the darkened window, his smile fading.

Mrs. Addison gets up. "Thank you so much for trusting your memories to us. When you're ready, you can decide when we'll celebrate your parents' lives. I can see they loved you very much."

"Call me when you decide." Jonas gets up. "I'd be honored to lead the ceremony for you. We can take the church van to the cemetery." Jose jumps up and hugs him. Compelled to do the same, I slide off the stool. At the last second, I put my hand out to shake his.

"May I say a prayer?" My voice is low, hesitant. A first for me. They gather around. "Jesus. Thank you for divine appointments. Amen."

I go into the den, too wound up to sleep. Looking out the window, I check for Chief Howell's car. Not home yet. I need to tell him how we met Justin and my suspicions about a drug delivery in Miami this weekend. It sounds bizarre, but stranger things have been happening. Hearing Jose come into the room, I turn to him. He drops onto the couch. Wow! He looks so grown up.

"I want to go see Mommy's and Poppy's graves soon, Pedro."

"Same. As soon as possible? I have a test on Wednesday. Thursday? There's no school Friday. It would be a long weekend off school."

Hopping up, Jose says, "I'll go ask Mom!" Within a minute, he's back. "She's making calls now and will let us know if Thursday works for everybody." He sits again, this time wrapping his arms around his middle. "I'm excited and a little scared."

"Yeah, it's like finally we can see Mommy's and Poppy's graves. We can say goodbye. I'm thankful we have the Addison family to go with us. And Jonas. We are blessed in that way." Okay, I'm finally getting what our family means when they claim they are blessed. Blessed is not a word I'd have used, not until tonight.

"Yeah. It was so miserable with Dee and the circus. Now we live in an actual home with actual parents who are planning to adopt us. But,

Pedro, you still seem out of it sometimes. Like you did at the circus. Far away. And you never tell me what's going on anymore."

"I do have something to tell you, Jose. Super serious stuff." I sit next to him and explain Andy's project to him. About Espinoza, Detective Andecker, the BMW, and Mommy's earring showing up. "Chief Howell is working with us."

"Wow! It's unbelievable that you guys have found out so much. How soon before he catches the killers?"

"Not soon enough. From now on, I'll tell you what's going on as things happen. For now, we must wait and be patient. Remember, the police are working on it. For me, that's the hardest part. Chief Howell won't disappoint us. Please don't tell anyone outside our house. That's important. For everyone's safety."

Jose nods.

Mrs. Addison comes to the doorway of the den and tells us the memorial is arranged for Thursday, just four days away. "We have much to accomplish. Family meeting after dinner tomorrow night," She announces.

Jose and I look at each other. I raise my eyebrows. What does 'much to accomplish' mean? Jose laughs and shrugs. I grin and hug him hard. Whatever! It is certain to be good. Jose pulls away, describing the special food he wants to make for the memorial. Mommy's favorite, caramel flan.

I have my own ideas. Upstairs, I knock on Sara's half-open door.

24

Chief's Request

S ara is Face timing with Danny again. Waving me in, she turns the phone to include me on her screen. I bring them up to speed about the memorial on Thursday.

"That's fantastic, Pedro! I'll bet Jose is thrilled. Count me in." Danny gives a thumbs up. Sara reaches over and hugs me. This is one huggy family.

"Will you please sing my mother's favorite hymn, Sara? It's '*Amazing Grace*.'"

"Of course!" She looks at me. "I know all the words. I hope I don't cry." Her eyes well up.

"Don't worry. Whatever you do will be perfect. Jose and I love your voice, and I'm positive my parents will hear you." My breath catches in my throat. "I'll leave you two. See ya in the morning, Danny. Oh, hey! Let Andy know about Thursday if you talk to him before I do."

"Will do. Later, dude."

One by one, the Addison family comes into the kitchen after dinner the next day to plan our memorial. Jose is pulling a fresh batch of chocolate chip cookies out of the oven. I pull out a chair next to me for Mrs. Addison. She smiles. I grin back. How did I not notice her kind gray eyes? It's as if I'm seeing her for the first time. The perfume she's wearing smells vaguely familiar. Across the counter, for the first time, I notice Luke's and Sara's eyes. They're a vivid blue. Sara is humming "Amazing Grace."

Luke is plugging a mini scanner into his computer. I move my packet of photos over. Mr. A. strolls in draped in the red, white, and blue lone star Cuban flag, singing the Cuban national anthem!

My throat catches, and I turn to Jose. Poppy hung our flag at the top of the stairwell in our townhome in Hialeah. Mr. A. can't carry a tune, but his singing is priceless. Jose and I stand and join in. As we finish, he passes the flag to us. Taking out his phone, he signals that he's going to take a picture. We pose, the rest of the family leaning in for a second shot.

Has somebody turned up the volume on the good things in my life? The love of the people in this room is overwhelming. I fold the flag and place it on the counter, motioning for Mr. A. to sit beside me. And just like that, I'm seated at the family dinner counter between my new parents. Taking a deep breath, I will this moment, this connection, to last. Jose crunches into a cookie.

"You sure did your homework, Dad." Luke laughs, busy scanning my photos in the order we set them up last night.

We agree that Thursday morning we'll meet at the church. Luke's slideshow will play on the welcome screen in the lobby. Sara will sing. Then Pastor and Jonas will perform the memorial service. We'll finish with Jose and me talking about our parents' lives.

Next, we'll eat brunch at Pastor's house, making our favorite Cuban dishes to honor our parents. Afterward, Jonas will drive us to the Ave Maria Cemetery to visit the gravesites. We'll invite Chief and Mrs. Howell, Danny, Andy, their parents, and Cheree. The planning draws us closer. I get up to close the kitchen window. The temperature is dropping.

Glancing across the yard, I look for Chief's cruiser. Where is he? It's after 9:00, and he still hasn't come home. All day with no word from him or Andy. I need to tell Chief how I met Justin Espinoza and my suspicions concerning a drug deal this weekend. Having vowed I'd keep no secrets from him is making me super uncomfortable. It's been two days since I met Justin and saw Espinoza. I don't want Chief to think I'm betraying his trust.

Grabbing my hoodie, I step onto the Addison's' wraparound front porch. On the porch, in the dark, my special place. My calm place. I've needed this every day lately. Walking back and forth, I peer into the lighted windows, checking out my new family as they carry out their nightly routines. Each one of these people is nothing short of amazing ... as if Mommy and Poppy handpicked a family for us since they can't be here. Time slows as I enjoy these moments ... giving me a sense of belonging, although I often feel like an outsider looking in.

I pace faster, my thoughts racing once again. I know it could end up being another rough night. Clenching and unclenching my fists inside the pockets of my hoodie, I shake my head to clear it. Feeling perfectly secure, loved, and cared for one minute, then anxious, angry, and alone the next is taking its toll on me, an emotional roller coaster with no controls ... while getting little sleep. Maybe a walk and a cigarette will settle me down, bring back the peace I experienced while sitting between the Addisons earlier. If not, I'll drink the last of the rum before I turn in for the night. I need to sleep.

Yes! Almost 9:30 and the headlights from Chief's car are finally sweeping a path across our yards as he turns into his driveway. Is it too late to bother him? He might have had a long day.

Chief sits on his stoop and motions me over. I cut across the short distance in seconds and sit next to him. "Whatever has you pacing the porch at ninety miles an hour, son?" Chief grins.

"I can't stop thinking about Detective Andecker and Espinoza and that whole deal. It really has me going," I blurt out.

"It has me going, too. What do you make of everything so far? Those two being related," Chief drawls, gnawing on a toothpick.

"Well, I need to tell you ... we found out something more." I hesitate.

"We? As in who?" Chief turns to me, saying nothing more.

"Luke, Sara, Danny, Cheree, and I."

Pulling out my cell phone, I tap the screen until the image of Justin appears. "I took this photo of Espinosa's son, Justin, at the swim meet Friday. Saturday night, when you and Andy drove to Hialeah, we all went downtown to catch a movie and hang out. I showed this to Sara, and she recognized Justin sitting alone on a bench at Tansy Park. Check out the unibrow, a defining feature." I pass my phone to Chief.

"Sara waved him over, and we introduced ourselves from the swim meet. Justin turned out to be a cool dude. He surfs too. He hung with us for a while, until Espinoza coasted up the street in his new car. I was within three feet of him! I stepped back into the shadows. He didn't see me. It all happened quick, Chief. I need you to know that none of this was my doing."

"Except showing the picture around, Pedro. Cell phones ... the tool of the devil!" Chief frowns. I pocket my phone. "You could have been in real danger. Our case, as delicate as it is, could have been blown." Chief looks away, lost in thought.

Now for the critical part. "There's more." Chief's head jerks. "Luke and Danny invited Justin to go surfing Sunday morning. He showed up around 9:00. I was inside Kelly's Diner when Espinoza dropped him off. Another friend ended up taking Justin to the Tri-Rail Station after breakfast so he could get back to Miami. We swapped phone numbers. Here's the interesting part: Luke invited Justin back to surf with us next weekend. Justin said he'd like to, but his dad was staying in Miami next weekend."

"So?"

"So, Luke, Danny and I were talking. We think there are too many people in Colombia who are coming back to Miami next weekend. Andecker, for one. We figured a drug shipment might be arriving. It kinda makes sense." As I say the words, they sound silly, as if I've been watching too much TV. I clamp my mouth shut.

Chief is silent. "So many minors involved in this case can only lead to trouble." Chief bites on his toothpick. Swallowing hard, I look down. I slide my hands into my pockets to warm them. Touching my phone, I pull it out to check for messages.

"Look, son. This is getting too close for comfort. I'm going to request that you check in with me any time you have contact with this Justin kid. Or anytime you leave Boca. I may ask you to sit tight at some point to keep you out of danger. We also don't want you guys blowing any advantage Andy and I may have in this case. Deal?" He holds out his hand.

"Deal." I shake it. "I also wanted to ask if you and Mrs. Howell would attend my parents' memorial this Thursday. We're having a small service and lunch at the church and then driving to Ave Maria Cemetery in Miami. Jose and I have never been to their graves."

"Thank you for inviting us, Pedro. I wouldn't miss it," Chief answers. We continue talking, discussing several of his past cases. Learning more about forensic science is one of my new passions. Chief sure is one clever dude.

25

Temptation

I meet up with Luke heading to the parking lot after my last class. He asks, "Did you get the text from Chief? He wants us to stop by his office ASAP. Danny can take us over since it's a group text, and he's on it."

I stare at my phone. There it is: COME TO MY OFFICE AS SOON AS YOU CAN. My stomach sinks. What happened since we talked last night?

My fingers shake as I text Sara: DID YOU GET THE TEXT FROM CHIEF?

Sara: YES, DANNY AND I ARE WAITING FOR YOU GUYS IN HIS CAR.

I slow my steps. Why does he need to see us? This can't be good. What if...

They usher us into Chief's office, and he shuts the door behind us. "I need each of you to know this case is officially off limits to you. I can't endanger your safety by providing you with updates. I can't have you reaching out to anyone involved, including Justin Espinoza. Pedro, I know this isn't what you want to hear. I'm sorry. Experience with these types of criminal cases tells me that events can get ugly in a hurry. Dangerous even. Recognize that we're following every lead we have to identify the man who killed your parents. Pedro, please let me know if and when you leave Palm Beach County. Questions?"

I have one. "What happened today for you to do a 180, Chief? Is there a break in the case?" My tone sounds sharper than I intended, but his decision isn't fair. Heat rises in my chest. I yank at my collar. Why is it so hot in here? How could he just cut me off?

"Again, Pedro, I know this is not what you want to hear. My decision is for the safety of everyone involved. Including Justin Espinoza." He faces me. "We're done here. Go get on with high school life." Turning, he opens the door, signaling the end of the meeting.

We file out. I'm last, dragging my feet. I turn to Chief. He's on the phone, scratching his left wrist again. We uncovered vital clues! He can't just blow me off like this. What's happening? I work to swallow the sour taste in my mouth. I'll call Andy later, see what his take on all this is.

True to his calling, Dr. Danny does his best to make me feel better, to smooth things over. "Hey! My mom made a fire lasagna last night. Let's go to my house and demolish the rest of it. Then we can study outside by the pool."

"Let's go." Luke slides into the back seat. "I won't lie, bro. I like your house!" Silent, I give them a half smile and climb in next to him. My swirling thoughts drown out their conversation as we ride the short distance to Danny's house.

Danny drives his car around a huge, circular driveway ... three, four times ... so fast we're smashed against each other. By the time he stops, we're all laughing hysterically. I get out and stare up at the massive glass windows, looking straight through the house to a sparkling blue pool and out to a dock on Boca Lake. A low whistle escapes my lips. Turning to me, Luke nods. So, this is what two distinguished doctors can afford. No wonder Danny is so nerdy with his studies. This is a lot to live up to.

Inside, I can't stop staring. Shiny marble floors. Signed art on every wall. A small oil painting of a clown face hanging in the entrance hallway doesn't bring up the usual instant revulsion. It's tasteful, with thick brushstrokes and pure color pigment. My art teacher would love to use this as an example of how to create an oil painting. We only have pictures from books to inspire us.

Sitting on a leather and chrome stool at a marble kitchen counter, I continue to look around while running my hand across the smooth polished surface. Amazing, bold objects of art are everywhere. Blown glass, bronze, and cool mixed media. Such a magnificent home! The windows looking out back show the lake water reflecting in the bright sun.

"We're having leftovers. Lasagna?" Sara opens the microwave. The smell of reheated lasagna hits me. Yes! I'm hungry.

If Danny's intention is to distract me from Chief's unwelcome news, he's doing a great job. Wow! These guys are the best of friends—my friends. They'll get me through this. I need to lean on them for support. That's the tough part. I glance at the clown picture. In the past, Big Dee was my support system.

We carry our food to the TV room and sit on a thick white carpet, putting our dishes on a round coffee table larger than any dining room table I've ever seen. Checking out the immense flat screen TV, I stare at the fully stocked bar next to it. Lucky you, Danny. You can take a secret sip whenever you need one.

"Hey, look, not a cloud in the sky!" Sara points out the window. "Let's get some sun before we have to go back for swim practice. We can study later."

"And a quick nap." Luke leads the way. "Let's skip swim practice. It'll be our first time. I can do laps in your pool, Danny."

I look around and point to the bathroom. "Be right out." On my way back, I stop for a closer look at the liquor cabinet. I glance toward the pool, then slip a lower cabinet door open, looking inside. There's a vast supply of unopened liquor bottles. Without thinking, I slip a bottle of rum into my backpack. I quickly cut through the living room and out to the patio deck. Realization hits me in my gut. I've swiped a bottle of liquor from the doctor who operated on me—for free. My stomach clenches. What a lowlife! A thief. Worse than Big Dee ever was. I'll put it back as soon as I can!

The afternoon drags by. My mind is all over the place, flipping be-tween self-loathing, then laser-focused, looking for a reason to go inside without seeming suspicious. There's a casita on the patio, a small BBQ kitchen with a refrigerator. I can't use the excuse of going inside the main house for a cold soda. The guest house also has a bathroom and is closer than the one inside. Finally, it's time to leave. We pile into Danny's car. With the bottle of rum.

The only one quiet on the ride home, I feel the need to say something as Danny drops us off. "Thanks, guys. You did it again. What did I do to deserve friends as amazing as you?" Clearly nothing.

"Friends always!" Danny high-fives me before putting the car into gear and taking off.

Alone in my bathroom, I stash the second stolen bottle in my secret spot, vowing to return it. There are so many bottles in their liquor cabinet. I hope the Wainwrights don't miss this one. Catching my reflection in the mirror, I stop to look myself in the eye for a long moment. I have to look away. Shame washes over me. Who am I? I didn't give in to the temptation to steal. I just did it. As if I'd pre-planned it. But I didn't! In an instant, I'd broken a commandment and dishonored Doc.

Now, more than ever before, I need a gulp of that rum! Making sure the bottle is well hidden in the cabinet, I close the door and turn to leave the bathroom, not able to look at myself in the mirror again.

I go downstairs to watch TV with Mr. A.

26

Going to the Mall

Finally! Wednesday afternoon and Sara, Danny, Luke, and I dash out to the student lot. Four days away from classes, teachers, swim and dive practice. No swim meet this Saturday. Luke gave the team today, tomorrow, and Friday off from practice. Mommy and Poppy's memorial is tomorrow, and we have lots to do, according to Mrs. Addison.

First on the list is to get us suits. Mommy bought us new suits every year for Easter. (We got new ones just before they were killed.) Then, the day after Easter, we'd go to a department store photo studio for a family portrait. Did she ever pick up the photos from the last time? Where are those suits today? Not that they'd fit. We've both grown a couple of sizes. It's strange having the Addisons buy our suits.

"Look what I have!" Luke waves Mr. A.'s debit card high in the air. "We're going shopping!" Putting the top of his convertible down, Danny joins the mass exodus of cars from the lot.

"To the mall! My favorite place!" Sara sings out. "Power shopping time!"

"Hey, it's a guys' trip. Dad said nothing about adding more clothes to your bulging closet. Today it's dudes only."

"You still need me to stand outside the dressing room and tell you if your colors match—or not," Sara teases.

"Maybe we'll let you help." Luke smiles. "What do you think, Pedro?"

"Since I haven't had new dress clothes in a while, I'll take all the help I can get. I don't know what size I am. Jose's grown too—a lot! It's great of your folks to do this for us. Jose said he'd be waiting in front of his school parking lot," I tell Danny.

"You got it." Danny slows for the school zone, then stops for Jose, who's waving at us from across the street. His latest favorite thing is to hop over the front door of Danny's convertible instead of opening the car door. He half-lands, half crashes into Sara on the front seat.

"Hey! Cool! I'm the man today, with my high school bros picking me up in a convertible!" He waves at his friends on the sidewalk.

Poppy always said Jose brought his special brand of sunshine wherever he went. I reach over and mess his hair. "Should we get matching suits? You remember, like Mommy always bought us? Or are we getting too old for that?"

He turns to me. "Let's do it one last time—in case they're watching from heaven tomorrow. Black?"

Swallowing hard, I nod my agreement.

Danny makes his way through the middle school crowd. "My favorite people are sitting in this car—and I'm responsible for your safety. Seatbelt." He nudges Jose, who has turned up the radio and is busy clowning around, waving to his friends.

"Hey, Danny, Andy said he's coming to the memorial tomorrow. He'll meet us at the cemetery in Miami," I call from the back.

"Great. I know it'll mean a lot to him, being there. You're family, Pedro. Ditto the feeling here, too, both you guys." Danny pats Jose on the arm. Sara hugs Danny a little tighter.

27

Memorial

The house is quiet as Jose and I dress for the memorial service. We tuck the remaining pages of Mommy's and Poppy's small, tattered Bibles into our new suit pockets. I straighten Jose's tie. He grabs me and pulls me in for a long hug. This is it. "Let's go!" Opening the bedroom door, we start down the stairs.

We're quiet as we eat breakfast. Afterwards, Sara comes in from her garden with a bouquet of roses and wraps them carefully for our trip to the cemetery. Jose, more hyper than the rest of us, checks the clock on the microwave often. As usual, I stand close when he gets like this.

"Wow! You guys look so grown up." Mrs. Addison claps her hands before adjusting our ties and cuffs, then hugs us. Such a mom! Thank You, Lord. Danny's signature knock sounds, and Sara goes to let him in. Danny, Chief, Mrs. Howell, and Jonas are standing behind him on the front porch.

"Your ride awaits you." Jonas smiles, gesturing toward the driveway. He brought the large white church van so we could ride together.

As we walk out to the porch, Sara holds up her hand. "Wait! Chief, please take our picture. This is an important day." She arranges everybody on the steps around Jose and me, steps into the group, then nods to Chief.

We climb into the van. "How Great Thou Art" is playing, setting the mood. Jonas says, "I know the cause for this memorial comes from a family tragedy, but I can't help but marvel at how God's hand has reached down and pulled us all together today. We're chosen to support you, Pedro and Jose. In your grief, please remember that—and to lean on us. I think your parents would approve, don't you?" Jonas looks at us in the rearview mirror.

"Oh, yes!" Jose leans forward, sitting on the edge of the seat. "If our parents were here, we'd all be great friends. Mrs. Addison, you and my mom are a lot alike, and my dad loved to design and build cool things with his hands, just like you, Mr. A." Jose points out the van window to the waterfall and set of small ponds at the end of the driveway under the sign that reads "Addison's Tree Farm."

"Why, thank you, Jose! I built that water feature when we opened our tree farm years ago. By getting to know you boys, I feel I know your parents in a small way. I'm confident we'd have liked them very much." Mr. A. put his arm around Mrs. Addison's shoulders—just like Poppy used to do.

I'm silent as we walk into the chapel. In the foyer, Luke slips the thumb drive into the TV so our slideshow will play continuously. On the altar, between two tall white candles, is a large copy of the only photo we have of our parents together. It takes my breath away.

Jose and I sit in the front row next to the Addisons. Pastor, Mrs. Thomas, Jonas, and Katie sit across from us. Cheree, Danny, and his parents sit behind us. Yes, we are safe, protected, and loved by these folks. They only wish the best for us. Family. I draw in a deep breath, still struggling to take it in. Miracles happen. This is evidence.

Sara starts singing "Amazing Grace," her clear voice making my eyes tear up. Bringing my arm around Jose's shoulders, I feel him inch closer. Next, Jonas begins speaking about Mommy and Poppy as best he can, piecing together the information we gave him the other night.

It's time for us to speak. I hope I can hold it together. Sara takes my hand and squeezes it. Thanks, sis! My heart swells as Jose stands tall and strides to the front. He looks so grown-up in his new suit. I draw in a sharp breath. So proud of you, little brother! You've been through so much. Thank You, God, that he survived it all.

Jose begins, "At Vacation Bible School, we learned God is love. I'm going to tell you what my parents loved because that's how I know they're with me. Mommy loved Poppy, and Poppy loved her. They both loved us. They loved God and Jesus, America, learning, eating, family, baseball, and taking long walks together." At this, he pauses, meets my gaze, then takes a shaky breath. That's what they were doing when they were killed. "Poppy loved building things, fixing broken things, and my mom's cooking. Mommy loved cooking, her garden, knitting, and sewing. She could skip stones across the water way farther than Poppy and loved to tease him about it. Whenever I hear or see people doing these things, I remember they are still with me—in my heart." Jose puts his hand over his heart and sits back down next to me.

I walk to the front. Can they see me now? Did they see me stealing that rum? How do I honor them when I'm so ashamed of who I've become? Taking a shaky breath, I begin, "Wow! That was perfect, Jose. I hope I don't spoil it by describing the things our mommy and poppy detested." Glancing from face to face, I continue, "As immigrants, they disapproved of arrogance, prejudice, injustice, bigotry, lies, fighting, and people speaking bad about each other. My parents were kind and generous people who deserve to still be with us. They'll always be alive in my heart." Turning, I stare at their photo for a long minute, a tear running down my cheek. I take my seat.

Mr. and Mrs. Addison step to the front. Mrs. Addison looks at us. "It seems you've been a part of our family for longer than just a few short weeks. We are thrilled that we'll spend the rest of our lives as your family, Pedro and Jose."

Mr. A. continues, "You bring so much to our home. Your heritage, likes, dislikes, values, and interests. Our family is indeed richer because you are with us. We will continue to honor Frank and Isabella Ramirez in our hearts. They can rest peacefully in heaven, knowing we will finish their good work," he ends, wiping a tear from his wife's cheek.

Pastor Thomas says a closing prayer, and we make our way to the lobby. We share our family memories with the others as our photos flash across the TV screen. The screen is so large and life-sized. It's as if Mommy and Poppy are right here. I want to reach out and hug them one last time. That will never be. This final realization almost chokes me, the lump in my throat huge.

"I'm hungry," Jose declares. "Mom disappearing can only mean one thing. They're bringing the food out!" He leads the way as we walk over to Pastor's house. On the sideboard is a feast of Cuban food: tortillas, salsa, black beans and rice, Chicharron chicken chunks, fried plantains, and salad. Jose's homemade pastelito desserts. Fancy puff pastries filled with tropical fruits are set out on a round table near the window. Our celebration ramps up as we eat and tell stories of the different holidays our families shared over the years.

I surprise them, and myself, by telling little-known facts of our Cuban ancestry. "The Ramirez family was of the Taino Indian tribe. Since Fidel Castro came into power, the few surviving tribe members organized, settling in Caridad de los Indios. It's a small, remote village. The Chief's name is Panchito Ramirez. The Taino tribe was assumed to have been extinct until recently."

"Wow, that's fantastic!" Jonas says. "I studied the Taino tribe in med school last semester. They grow rare, useful herbs for medicine. What else do you know about the Taino?"

Jose grins. "Mommy and Poppy said to always speak about our people. Lots of our traditions aren't written down and talking about them is how our history stays alive. They call it oral history. Chief Ramirez is a healer and herbalist. The tribe has about 400 Indians who still live in huts called bohitos. The roofs are thatched, tightly woven palm fronds to make them waterproof. The Taino's preserve their healing forest on a small island in the Toa River, high in the mountains of Cuba."

I nod. "Hundreds of medicinal plants grow there. They're organic because there is no need for chemicals. These herbal plants are called green medicine and are becoming known worldwide."

"Yes, yes! I've heard of this," Doc says. "It's amazing! Are you boys related to Chief Panchito Ramirez?"

I grin. "Ramirez is one of the most common Cuban names. I don't know, sir."

"But we would be welcome in the village because we have Taino Indian blood in us," Jose adds.

28

Ave Maria Cemetery

Back to Miami, but this time it's for Mommy and Poppy. To say goodbye. Is this the closure Jonas was talking about the other night? If closure is relief from the constant pain that plagues my thoughts, I'll take it. Rolling my head sideways on the headrest, I look over at Jose, who is fast asleep. I need to find that peace, the peace I see in his sleeping face. Danny's parents and the Thomases stayed in Boca since they had previously scheduled appointments.

The tires crunch as Jonas turns into the small cemetery parking lot. Andy's waiting for us in his Jeep. Our new family and friends truly care. It seems so. A new beginning. Is the worst of this nightmare finally behind us?

"Hey, Andy. Thanks for coming. It means a lot." I shake his hand. Yeah, it's a little formal, but this occasion is special.

"I wouldn't miss it." He smiles, giving Jose a high-five and Danny a hug.

Jonas, Chief, and I go inside to get directions to the gravesites. The rest crowd inside the small lobby behind us. The temperature dropped since we left Boca. Another winter cold front is expected to blow in this afternoon.

Jonas smiles at the receptionist sitting behind the counter. "We'd like directions to the gravesites of Frank and Isabella Ramirez, please."

The receptionist taps on her computer, then looks up at Jonas. "I'm sorry, sir. Only one Ramirez is buried in this cemetery. Isabella Ramirez. Right here." Her finger lands on a spot on a map on the counter.

Jonas says, "There's a Frank Ramirez as well. They were buried on the same day."

She pages back through a cemetery logbook, then points to a date. "No, sir, there was only one burial on that day. See?" She then turns the book around on the counter for us to see. "I'm sorry if there has been a misunderstanding..."

Chief and Andy glance at each other. Frozen to the spot, I shake my head, pressing my fists to both eyes. Dropping my hands to my sides, I step over to the book to be certain that what she is saying is true. This isn't possible. I open my mouth to say something, then snap it shut. There's nothing to say. Right there! It's written in black and white: Isabella Ramirez, buried on May 12, 2022. My arm instinctively slips around Jose's shoulders.

"Where's my father buried?" Jose asks the woman. "Another cemetery?"

"Honey, I don't know." The woman looks from Jose to me, shaking her head. Andy walks to the exit, phone to his ear.

"We'll go to your mother's gravesite. Let's not forget why we're here." Mrs. Addison leads us, opening the door and holding it for us. A blast of cold air fills the room. Silently, we follow Jonas, walking the short distance to a grave marked with a small grave marker lying flush to the ground. It reads, "Isabella Ramirez, 1995 ~ 2022." Bright red and white impatiens grow above the stone. Jose and I kneel together.

He looks as stunned as I feel and silently rubs his hand across the letters on Mommy's headstone, as if to bring her back to us. Numb, my thoughts won't come together. I stand, blinking and shaking my head to clear the ringing in my ears. This can't be possible... I don't understand... What happened to Poppy's body?

Mr. A. holds out his hands, and everyone circles around us. "Father in heaven, we celebrate the life of Isabella Ramirez. Give rest to her soul and take care of her two sons. Help us love and care for them as Isabella did. In this way, we honor her and Frank. In Jesus's name we pray. Amen."

Jose stands and Sara hands each of us a rose. One by one, we set them in a vase mounted on the rear of the stone.

Well, that was a fine prayer for Mommy. But what about Poppy? Is his body at the bottom of some murky, polluted canal in the Everglades? His death certificate is at home, in my dresser drawer. I should have brought it. A lot of good that would do now. I cling to Jose, who is sobbing hysterically. Holding back the tears, my throat aches, my body tense and tight as I clench and unclench my fists. How do I handle this fresh fury inside? I stare at the grave, at the small engraved marker. Squeezing my eyes shut to clear my vision, I feel a tear wet my face.

Lifting my chin, I swipe the tear aside. Someone, please break the horror of this moment. Everybody's watching us. Stop touching me. Stop gawking at me like some freak in a circus. Get away! It's all wrong. Wrong. wrong, wrong! It will never be right. Mommy and Poppy are dead! But where is Poppy?

"Aaahhhhh!" I look at the sky, crying out in agony. The raw sound that fills the air startles me, but not enough to make me stop. Again and again, I howl, months of misery erupting from my deepest places. Jose and I sink to the grass on Mommy's grave, weeping for a long while. Eventually, I suck in my breath, finally feeling nothing. Spent. Numb. Life would be bearable if I could deal with this numbness with rum. At least for a time.

"Pedro?" Jose takes my face with both hands. *"God is a safe place to hide, ready to help when we need him.* Mommy used to sing that to us. Remember?" I put my arm around his shoulders, staring at the grass surrounding the gravestone and he leans into me. Pulling some grass aside, I clean it off the stone, then trace Mommy's name with my baby finger. I miss you so much. Strength seeps back as I think about the words Jose recited. Psalm 46. How many times did we sit while Mommy read that psalm aloud to us? Life was hard for our family. Cuban immigrants with no other family to lean on. Poppy always said that we had to lean on God. But where did God go? Where is Poppy? Sara hums a familiar melody, warming up her voice.

"He is here..." Her clear voice ring outs, filling the air. "Almighty Father God, He is here. Faithful hand of God, You are here..." I look up, a small hope replacing my numbness. The faces of the people who are changing our lives are gathered around Mommy's grave. They never met her ... but they're here. My desperation dissolved, replaced by... what? Hope? Hope for a future, even if it is without Mommy and Poppy? Maybe so... Do I dare trust this hope? Clasping my hands in prayer and dropping my chin on them, I whisper, "Please, Lord." Jose and I stand. Soon we're all hugging, drying each other's wet cheeks.

Andy reaches into his pocket, pulling out his phone. Chief and Andy huddle together, looking at the screen. After endless minutes of tapping and scrolling, Chief looks up at the sky. Staring at him, I wait for him to speak, my earlier tension returning full force. He looks at Jose and me.

"While there is a record of your mother's death, there is no record of your father's death. There is no record of your father, period. Anywhere. He's vanished. We're checking hospital records now." He glances at Andy, who, while tucking his phone into his pocket, shakes his head.

"Well, that is the ultimate injustice." I stalk off toward a small, still pond in the middle of the cemetery. Jose, Luke, and Danny catch up with me. We stand side by side for a time, not speaking, looking out across the water. The wind picks up. Massive, black, billowing clouds swirl above us. Rain's coming. I stoop in the gravel, chose a flat stone, then skip it across the water. One, two, three, four skips. Again. Another. Soon the four of us are trying to outdo each other, skipping stones, laughing, and high-fiving. The tension has broken.

The others are in the van, probably trying to stay warm. We join them. "How do we find our father?" I ask Chief Howell, my voice flat, matter of fact. "Is he dead or still alive?" That's the question nobody is asking.

"I don't have the answer to that, son. You can bet I won't sleep much until I find out," Chief says. "Andy, can you drive me to Hialeah and then drop me off at the Tri-Rail Terminal? I need to turn up some answers today, need to see the spot where the Ramirezes were run down." Today, yes! This is good. Chief is rubbing the inside of his wrist with his thumb. He reaches into the van and retrieves his bag. "I also need someone who is fluent in Spanish. Your roommate, maybe?"

"Esta mio. Vamos!" I say, jumping out of the van. Chief stiffens, then turns at me, a look of doubt on his face. Time to be my most convincing. I need to be in on Chief's plan. "I know Hialeah like the back of my hand—and where all my parent's friends lived. They might know something. They'll trust me and tell me things they'd never tell you. Cubanos are a tight-knit community."

Chief looks at Andy, who nods. "That's true, sir. Cubans must stick together, support each other."

"What do you think?" Chief asks Mr. and Mrs. Addison. I hold my breath.

"Will he be safe? Where are you going?" Mrs. Addison asks.

"Yes, he'll be safe. I want to start at the scene of their parents' accident and then go wherever that leads us," Chief says. "We could hit a bunch of dead ends and be home within a couple of hours."

"He has our permission." Mr. A. looks at his wife, who nods in agreement.

I let out my breath. "Chief, I know every reason you don't want me to join you guys. I promise to remain as calm and professional as you and Andy. I promise!"

Chief smiles. "I'll hold you to that, son. Step out of line, we'll cut it short and head home. Understand?"

"I understand." Poppy is alive. I know it. I can help find him. I hug Jose before climbing into the back of Andy's Jeep.

"Find Poppy, Pedro. Every November he planted red and white impatiens in Mommy's front garden."

29

Evidence

"If I repeat myself, I'm sorry, guys. Speaking out loud is how I gather my thoughts and sort matters out. Speak up and add your ideas. Let's start from the beginning." I watch Chief quickly page through papers in his case. "Okay, let's travel back in time. Today, we are the Hialeah police. We just received a call about a hit and run at this address." He copies the address onto his phone. "Let's go. Our complication is that we have no evidence and what little there was, is now missing."

"If evidence isn't collected, it can't be analyzed," Andy says. "Which also works for a crooked cop trying to bury the truth."

"Exactly! This is it. Let's get our bearings here. The accident was on the south side of the street, which means the driver ran the car up over that sidewalk, somewhere along there." Chief points to a row of shops with only a narrow sidewalk between the building and the busy street. "There's a sandwich shop, a pharmacy, and a check cashing store. All two-story buildings. Doctors' and law offices on the top floor. Let's ask if anyone remembers the accident." Andy parks the Jeep. Chief heads toward the pharmacy. "Least likely to go out of business in eighteen months," I overhear him mutter.

"My parents used to shop at this pharmacy." My breathing comes fast. "They were good friends with the owners, Mr. and Mrs. Rodriguez." I hold the door and follow Chief and Andy inside the small, one-aisle pharmacy. The familiar smell of rubbing alcohol and penny candy hit my nose. I look inside the candy counter and see some of Jose's and my old favorites.

Chief Howell introduces himself to the pharmacist, whose bright eyes darken when Chief asks if he recalls the Ramirez hit and run accident. Mr. Rodriguez looks past Andy and spots me.

"Pedro? Pedro Ramirez?" His eyes grow wide as I grin, stepping forward. We hug, speaking rapidly in Spanish. Mr. Rodriguez grows serious as I ask him to answer Chief's questions. I formally introduce everyone.

"Yes, of course I tell all I see on this terrible night." His broken English is typical of many immigrants. His Cuban accent, music to my ears after being away for so long. Too long.

"May I record our conversation and video the area, sir?" Chief asks. Andy pulls equipment from Chief's bag.

"Yes, of course. This couple are my good customers. And my friends. They are fine, God-fearing people. First, I hear a loud popping noise and then a car crash. I rush to this window." He leads us to the large plate-glass window at the front of the store. "It happens right there, not more than ten feet away." He points to the spot where the accident took place. "That nice lady, I called her Issa, that's Cuban nickname for Isabella. She lay lifeless, like a rag doll, right there on the sidewalk."

My stomach turns as I stare at the pavement outside the window. So, this is where it happened. Right here. I imagined it so many times, in so many ways. This makes it real. Worse than I ever imagined. Tears burn my eyes. I look over at Mr. Rodriguez, who reaches over, puts his arm around my shoulder, and squeezes. He doesn't let go. I swipe away my tears. Focus ... focus on today ... now ... I will make this right, Mommy.

In a gentler tone, Mr. Rodriguez continues, "Next, I run to the phone by the register to call the police. I notice a police car out front before I even pick it up. The lights were flashing, and the officer was kneeling over her. Before he comes inside, he runs around the back of the building. Probably looking for the car that hit Issa. I don't know why she walks alone that day. Issa and Frank always walked together every evening." Chief glances at Andy, who is taking notes.

We step outside. "I recall the accident like it happen yesterday. Horrible! The detective say the loud, popping noise ... it perhaps a tire blowing out which cause the car to skid out of control, up onto pavement. The detective ask a few peoples questions, including me. Not many peoples were out because it start to rain. An ambulance come about twenty minutes later and take Issa. That's the last I see of her. I always wonder if they capture the person who kills her. Her husband, Frank, never come by after that. I can see why, too. Bad memories."

"Did you see the automobile that struck her?" Chief asks.

"Yes, a big dark blue BMW with dark windows. Then it is gone. There is broken glass here on the sidewalk. That policeman sweep it into this drain grate." He points down at the grate, then to a spot on the wall. "The car hit the building right here. The police are very kind to come and paint this wall for me the very next morning." Mr. Rodriguez runs his hand over the white wall. He holds up his palm. It's covered in a white chalky substance. "Too bad, cheap paint."

"Do you remember anything else that might help us, Mr. Rodriguez? Did the detective who questioned you give you his card?" Chief asks.

"Yes, I ask for it. Twice, if I remember correctly. I put it in the cash register." He leads us back inside, calling out in Spanish. A woman comes from the back of the store. She opens the drawer and hands Chief a card.

"This is my wife, Mrs. Rodriguez. She was also friendly with Frank and Issa. Look! It's Pedro Ramirez!" The woman cries out and gives me a tight hug.

"Detective Andecker," Chief reads the card. He holds it by its edges as Andy pulls out a vial. Chief drops the card inside. Andy snaps the cap shut, recording the information on the label.

"May I ask you and your wife a few more questions?" Chief asks.

"We try to help all we can. After that night, nobody ever come. Like nothing bad ever happen." Mr. Rodriguez shakes his head, throwing his hands in the air. "Poof!"

"Did your call go through to the police station when the accident happened?"

"No, no! The police car is already out front. So, I just hang up," he explains.

"Was there blood?" Chief asks gently, casting a glance my way. I'm doing okay and nod for him to continue.

"Yes, blood here on the sidewalk and on this wall." Mr. and Mrs. Rodriguez lead us outside, pointing to a section on the pavement and white wall. Andy records everything. Chief reviews a few previous questions for clarification.

"Where did they sweep the glass?"

"Right here. All into this sewer drain."

"How many law enforcement cars and vans showed up?"

"Only one. With Detective Andecker."

"Was there a crime scene van or any other police vehicles?"

"No. And after, I think that is unusual. On TV, there are always lots of cars and trucks and flashing lights. That night, just one car, one police officer. He was very efficient and finish his work quickly. Twenty minutes later, ambulance comes to take poor Issa away. We read about it in the paper the next day. They say Frank is killed, too, but you know how newspapers always make mistakes."

"Yes. We are also looking for Frank Ramirez. Did you see Frank later that day or afterwards?" Chief asks.

"No, sir. I was concerned because he buy his heart medicine from me, and I know he require it."

Chief looks up. "Heart medicine?"

"Yes, he have high cholesterol. Once a month he refill his prescription," Mrs. Rodriguez chimes in.

"Do you have his doctor's name and address?" Chief slows his words, as if trying not to sound too excited.

"Sure. Maybe it helps?" She takes us back inside and writes the information on a slip of paper. "Dr. Velez has an office a few buildings down. We referred Frank to him a few years ago. Here is our card and phone number in case we can help more." She turns to me and puts her hands on my shoulders. "You are our friends! Please, tell your Poppy to come visit us when you find him."

"You have been a great help," Chief says. "I have one more question, and I need you to consider carefully before you answer. Did you both hear the loud pop before the car crashed into the wall?" They both nod. "Can you identify that noise as anything other than a tire blowing out?"

"Maybe a gunshot. It was very loud. We hear gunshots in the neighborhood sometimes. Yes, it sounded like a gunshot. I have never heard a tire blowing out. So, I just trust the detective to know what he talks about. It make sense when he said it," Mrs. Rodriguez adds, looking at her husband. "Now that I think of it, the blue car drive away fast. No flat tire."

"Thank you so much for your time. Is it all right if we walk around the building?" Chief asks.

"Yes, of course." Mr. Rodriguez squeezes my arm. "Find Frank. Tell him we miss him." The pharmacist puts his arm around his wife, walking us to the door.

Mrs. Rodriguez stops at the candy counter and pulls out two long strips of Dots. "Su favorito. I remember, Pedro. Give one to Jose. Come see us. We miss you." Unable to speak, I nod, pocket the Dots, and hug them both.

Outside, Chief turns to us. "Well, my wrist has stopped itching. It looks as if we're up against a successful cover up. What do you think, Andy?" Andy nods as he continues to video. "Do you know anyone with an infrared camera?"

"My roommate has one. Should I call him?"

"If he could get here as soon as possible, that would help determine what's behind that cheap paint. We also need to locate a small thing called a bullet," Chief answers. "That would tie this thing together nicely. Let's walk to the back of the building and see if we can find our way to Dr. Velez's office from there. As if we are wounded from a bullet and running from our killer." Chief is speaking to himself once again as he leads us into the alley.

We stop abruptly, staring at a labyrinth of alleys, paths, and porticos that lead in at least six different directions. Dumpsters clutter the narrow alleys, almost blocking the way through.

I lead the way until I find the door to a short flight of stairs leading to Dr. Velez's office. It's an old building with a dim hanging bulb at the end of the hallway. At the top of the stairs are two doors. Chief knocks on the one that reads "Dr. Velez."

30

Dr. Velez

A short, older woman opens the door to Dr. Velez's waiting room. Chief shows her his badge, asking to speak with the doctor. She steps back, her face turning pale.

Looking past Chief, she sees me in the hallway. "Pedro! Raul, come quick! It's Pedro Ramirez!" I step inside the room, and she hugs me like she would never let go. Dr. Velez walks in, opening his arms wide.

"Pedro, mi hijo!" I embrace the doctor, who is now much shorter than I am. "You've grown! You are today a man. Where is Jose?" He looks past me.

"Jose's in Boca Raton, where we are living now." The waiting room has the familiar smell of coffee and cigars.

"Come in, come in. This is an incredible day. You are back, my son. You must inform us how you are and where you've been. Come in, come in. Please sit." He gestures to the chairs in his small waiting room. "Pedro, who are your friends? I am Dr. Velez," he introduces himself, holding out his hand. Chief and Andy shake hands as I introduce them. "This is my lovely wife, Mrs. Velez, Chief Howell and Andy Wainwright," Dr. Velez says.

Mrs. Velez asks us if we want some café Cubano. Smiling wide, I nod. "Si, Si, por favor... It's been a long time!"

As she leaves, Andy says, "Chief, you are in for a treat. Mrs. Velez is making us some authentic Cuban coffee. It's amazing!"

"I am pleased to meet friends of our Pedro. Please sit with us and enjoy our favorite time of day, afternoon coffee." She beams, setting a small tray with five tiny plastic cups on the coffee table. The strong coffee smell fills the room. Closing my eyes, I inhale, then take a sip, remembering Mommy teaching me step by step how to make perfect café Cubano. After school and before Poppy came home from work was our special time together. She would play lively Latino music and teach me complicated salsa dance steps.

"Delicious!" Chief's comment yanks me out of my memory. "I still don't get what the English think is so wonderful about afternoon tea." How does he know that in the Latin American culture, it's impolite to talk business right away? It's our custom to exchange pleasantries first.

"Not when you can drink cafe Cubano." Andy empties his cup. He stands to look at the doctor's diplomas hanging on the wall. "I see you graduated from the University of Miami School of Medicine. My father and mother also graduated from there."

"Do they practice in Miami?" Dr. Velez asks.

"No, they live in Boca Raton. I can't recall the exact year they graduated. Sometime around 1980, I think."

Dr. Velez laughs. "I was ten years ahead of them in school then. It's an excellent school. My son is a student there now."

"So am I," Andy replies.

"Is your son following in your footsteps and studying medicine?" Chief asks.

"No, he's learning filmmaking. And you?" Dr. Velez asks Andy.

"Forensic science," Andy replies.

"Ah! Does that have something to do with your visit today, Pedro?" The doctor smiles at me.

Before I can speak, Chief leans forward and launches into a summary of the cold case. "We're investigating the double murder of Frank and Isabella Ramirez." Instantly, the doctor's smile fades, and he takes a slow sip of his coffee. Chief was ready. "As you can see from my card, I am the Chief of Police in Boca Raton, Florida."

"Yes. You are a long way from home," Dr. Velez answers.

"Pedro and Jose Ramirez are personal friends—and next door neighbors." Dr. Velez looks at me as I nod. "Today we went to Ave Maria Cemetery, west of here. There was only one grave, Isabella Ramirez's. You can imagine Jose's and Pedro's shock."

"Yes. But why would they think their father is buried there?" Dr. Velez asks.

"They were told this by County Child Services the same night as the hit and run. The boys were picked up and taken to a group foster care home. They were told the same car killed both parents that night. It was further reported in the newspaper. The boys have death certificates for both their mother and father. Pedro and Jose ran away from the foster care system within weeks of their parents' deaths."

"Yes. This I know." Dr. Velez lays his hand on my arm and squeezes it.

Chief cocks his head, lifting his eyebrows, but continues, "They joined a traveling circus and hid out there for roughly a year and a half. The owner, who abused them mentally and physically, traumatized the boys. They are now safe, living in a decent Christian home, attending school, and eating three nutritious meals a day. The family they're living with is adopting them—"

"No!" Dr. Velez shouts, pushing up from his chair. "Their father, Frank, he is not dead!"

My heart freezes, then pounds. "Yes!" I gasp. Is this where Chief was leading the conversation. He's a real pro!

31

The Truth for Now

"What?" These are the words I was waiting to hear. "What are you saying, Dr. Velez? Poppy is alive?"

"Yes, Pedro. Yes!" He turns to me. "I don't know where Frank is now, but I can tell you that yes, he is alive." I slump in my chair, elbows on my knees, my head in my hands. My hair falls over my hands as I stare at the floor. Too much to hope for... Poppy is alive! Sobbing, I get up and hug the doctor, then Mrs. Velez.

Pulling away, I wipe my eyes on my sleeve. "Please tell us everything you know."

"Yes, of course," Dr. Velez begins. "The evening of the auto accident, your father was shot. He saw his poor Isabella lying dead on the sidewalk, crushed from the car that had brutally taken her life. Your father escaped, thinking only of you and Jose, of your safety. Frank knew you'd be in immediate danger. He ran around the back of the pharmacy and into the alley to hide. When he realized how bad his gunshot wound was, he made his way here."

Dr. Velez continues, "By the time Frank got here, he was weak from losing so much blood. More than that, he was out of his mind with grief and worry. I wanted to take him to the hospital, but he said no, he needed to get to you and Jose. I offered to call the police. He refused, saying it was a police officer who was involved in murdering your mother. That night, we did the only thing we could for him, remove the bullet and bandage him up." Dr. Velez looks at his wife, who shakes her head, yes.

"Where was he shot?" Chief asks. Andy is busy taking notes.

"The bullet lodged in his left arm. Luckily, it was in the upper part, where he was all muscle. He laid heavy block for a living. The muscle stopped the bullet, but his arm still bled a lot." The doctor pointed to a primary artery in the upper arm of a human-sized body chart on the wall.

"Then what happened?" My breath is coming faster.

"He was weak but insisted on going back to your house right away. At about 8:00 that evening, after I finished bandaging him up, Frank left. That was the last time we saw him. We watched the news for information. They said your father was dead from the hit and run! A couple of weeks later, there was something on the news about two boys the same ages as you and Jose who went missing from the foster care facility. We wondered if it could be you. They hush-hushed that story quick because of the terrible publicity for the county foster care system."

"Did you ever report Frank Ramirez's bullet wound to the police?" Chief asks.

Dr. Velez glances at Andy, who is still taking notes. He looks away and grows quiet. Chief Howell plucks the pen from Andy's hand. Andy puts his pad away.

Chief leans in again and says quietly, "Dr. Velez, I am here on behalf of Pedro and Jose. Only three hours ago, they went to visit their parents' graves for the first time and discovered only one parent. This is purely off the record. If you didn't report it to the police, that turned out to be a good thing for Frank Ramirez and his sons. It has kept them all safe from the person responsible for killing the boys' mother. I've been working on this case for only a week. I sincerely believe, with their father, that there is a dirty police detective responsible for the death of Frank's wife—and other crimes. I need all the help I can get to follow up on this cold case. Will you help us?" He puts Andy's pen in his shirt pocket.

Dr. Velez studies each of our faces for a long minute. He looks over to his wife, who gives a slight nod. "Okay, here is the truth of what happened that night. No, Chief Howell, I didn't call the police.

After dark, I drove Frank to his house. We spotted a car sitting a few houses down from Frank's, and Frank recognized it as a car from the house where he'd been working that day. Where all the trouble began. Frank's townhouse was dark. So, we continued driving down the street. I brought Frank back to our house."

"That night we watched the late news, and they reported on the hit and run. It showed the Child Services people taking Pedro and Jose from their home. Frank became hysterical. Who could blame him? He had witnessed the brutal death of his wife, and now his two boys were being snatched away. I gave him a sedative. We put him in our guest room to sleep." Dr. Velez looks past us and out the window, seeming to relive that night.

"What happened next?" Chief gently prompts.

"The next morning, he was gone. That's the last we saw of him. That is the truth, Chief Howell," Dr. Velez states.

"And the bullet? Where is it?" Chief saved the most important question for last. "The bullet is concrete evidence linking the shooter to the death of Isabella Ramirez.

"I put it in a plastic bag and told him to hold on to it. I told him it was his 'get out of jail free' card in case anything should happen to him with these bad people."

Chief sits back. He is silent, his brow furrowed. What is he thinking?

"Where would Frank Ramirez have gone that morning?" Chief finally asks, more to himself than anyone in the room. His question goes unanswered. He gets up and digs in his pocket for a business card. "You've been very helpful, Dr. and Mrs. Velez. This information changes everything. Here's my card with my number. If you think of anything else, please call."

"I will, Chief Howell. Before you go, Pedro, will you please tell us what happened after you ran away from the foster care facility? We were so worried ... you and Jose were my patients for many years."

I begin my story of traveling with the circus and Big Dee. I read the pain and sympathy on their faces as I tell them of the abuse Jose and I endured. I assure them we are safe in God's hands now with the Addison family, describing our new schools, church, and friends.

"Andy's father operated on my hands. Look, Dr. Velez, they're healed ... normal looking!" Grinning, I hold out both hands for his examination. Dr. Velez takes them and smiles his approval.

Andy adds, "My mom's an eye surgeon and will be operating on Jose in a few weeks. Right now, he's getting used to wearing corrective glasses. Mrs. Addison, the mother they're staying with, is tutoring him, and so far, he's getting good grades in school this year."

"I'll bring the boys down to visit once we catch the person or persons who killed their mother," Chief promises, getting up to leave.

While we wait in Andy's Jeep for his roommate, I try to process what I've heard so far, feeling much less tortured than earlier today.

Andy's roommate drives up, and Chief points out the area on the wall that needs to be photographed. "If we're lucky, the blood from Frank's arm will show through the paint as a black smear or spatter in the infrared photograph. I can't think of any other reason Andecker would have come himself and painted that wall the next day. I'm still furious that the broken glass from the headlight was immediately swept into the sewer, the gunshot wasn't written up in the official police report, and Frank Ramirez was reported as dead. One fact remains: Frank Ramirez won't be completely safe until Detective Andecker and his sidekick, Craig Espinoza, are in police custody. I'm sure your dad knows that, too."

My mind is whirling with the possibility of finding Poppy. Keeping himself so well hidden from Andecker also keeps him hidden from us. How will Chief proceed? Jose will be so happy tonight. Poppy, where are you?

32

Hialeah Police Station

Chief turns to Andy. "Do you have time for one more stop?"

"Sure. Where to?"

"The Hialeah police station. While Andecker is out of town, I'd like to meet again with the Hialeah Chief."

We pull into the station parking lot, and Chief says, "You'll both have to wait in the Jeep. I hope you understand." Nodding, I slump back in my seat. Chief is doing all he can, but I hate being left out.

"This is absolutely the work I want to do when I graduate." Andy sounds pumped. "Working on this case removes any doubt I might have had."

"Yeah? Why?"

"When you solve a case like this, it can't take the pain people have been carrying around go away, but it provides answers, and relief of not knowing. Take you and Jose, for instance. Tracking the evidence has led us right to where we are now and will eventually lead us to your dad. All that suffering will be in the past as you, Jose, and your dad are reunited. Then you can mourn your mother's death together and return to your lives as a family."

"I don't dare think that way, Andy. I gave up on that hope a long time ago. For now, I need to be content with how great life is with the Addisons. This way of life is safe today. I found out the hard way that hope can be a cruel liar." Rubbing my palm with my thumb, I think for a few minutes, then look at Andy. "Do you seriously expect this investigation to lead to my father? In this enormous city? Seems impossible. More than impossible." I close my eyes. Please, Lord.

"It could flush him out. Picture this plausible scenario: your dad realizes none of you will be safe until Andecker and Espinoza are behind bars. Think about it, Pedro. It's possible he has a plan to make that happen."

"Yeah, you're right." My words come out slowly. "You're right—or he could be dead." Poppy always had a long-term plan for our family. He was focused on our future. It makes sense he would have a plan to get us back together. What is it, Poppy? Where are you today? Are you safe? Are you alive?

Chief returns to the Jeep with a smile on his face. He describes his meeting. "The Chief was surprised, stating he didn't expect to see me again so soon. I asked if he'd located the lost evidence box. Embarrassed, he said they were still searching for it." He turns to Andy. "Years of experience and intuition tell me that this man is honest, an excellent public servant. Choosing to skip straight to the core, I took out your notepad, Andy, where you had so meticulously detailed this afternoon's interviews. As I presented the additional facts, I could see he realized the roles Andecker and his brother-in-law played. I'm pleased to report that the chief's reaction was a powerful mixture of anger and disgust."

Chief continues, "I told him that was why I needed to see him tonight, before Andecker returns from his Colombian vacation. That my hunch is that Andecker and his homeboys are bringing back a drug shipment from Bogota, Colombia, this weekend. However, I told him that this wasn't the primary reason for tonight's visit. Identifying those guilty of Isabella Ramirez's murder could lead to identifying members of the drug ring. It was a hunch, one worthy of serious consideration."

Chief stops for a minute, rubbing his chin, looking out the window. Turning back to us, he says, "He took it all in. On his desk was a framed photograph of his two sons in blue baseball uniforms. I picked the frame up and told him, 'Pedro and Jose Ramirez are the same ages as your boys. They were robbed of their parents and the chance to do the normal things youths their age do.' I then told him I was counting heavily on him to do all within his jurisdiction to make matters right for you two.

That I believed your father will come out of hiding when he learns the man who murdered his wife has been arrested. Then I asked for his help, chief to chief. He pledged it, along with the full cooperation of his police force. I trust him. We're in excellent hands."

On the return trip to Boca, my mind races as fast as the train we're traveling on. "You laid a lot of information and responsibility on the police chief in Hialeah."

"Yes. I also recognized that the concern of the Hialeah Department would be the drug shipment with the resulting arrests of Detective Andecker and Espinoza. Your mother's homicide would be an added charge brought against them. Hopefully, this news will bring your dad out of hiding, wherever he is. There are no more leads for me to pursue." Chief rubs the inside of his wrist as he nods off to sleep.

It has been a long day. Chief stops in at our house before heading home. We finish the leftovers from lunch as we bring everyone up to speed on the roller coaster events of the afternoon.

"So, all's well that ends well?" Mrs. Addison raises her eyebrows, looking at Jose and me.

"It hasn't ended yet." I smile, still riding high in the hope of having Poppy back.

"Well, I suppose that says it all for now." Chief grins. "Good night, folks."

33

Despair

Jose's faint snores, familiar and peaceful, should settle me. Not tonight. I lie wide awake, my mind churning over the day's events. Is Poppy alive? I stare wide-eyed at the ceiling. The shadow of the palm tree races back and forth in the wind. Once again, my mind is racing along with it.

I need to find him. Locating someone in a city as enormous as Miami is hopeless. Especially if they don't want to be found. What if Andecker found and killed him already? Eighteen months is plenty of time for a cop with endless resources to stalk and kill someone. Especially someone who is a major threat, like Poppy. He knew too much about these drug dealers. What if he is dead on the bottom of some murky canal in West Dade? We'll never find him.

How did this happen to my family? Why? The promise of this afternoon's discoveries drains away. Sliding off the bed, I slump to the floor, rolling my head back and forth on the side of the mattress. My world crumbles, turning ink black again. I was better off this morning when I thought both Mommy and Poppy were dead.

Tears drip into my clenched fists. I shake them off, punching fiercely into the air. Why, God? If You're such a loving God, why did you let Mommy be killed by drug traffickers? Why did You force Poppy to live without us for so long? Where is he today? Where are you now, God? I need you more than ever. Moaning, I swallow hard, trying to clear the awful thickness in my throat.

Getting up, I creep into the bathroom. The sure way to get rid of this lump in my throat and the pain in my heart is sitting under the white towels. My fingers meet the neck of the bottle of stolen rum. I unscrew the lid and take a long drink. Then another. And a third. Who's counting? The liquor burns its way down my insides. My red-rimmed eyes peer back at me from the medicine cabinet mirror.

Still tense, I throw my jacket on and pat my pocket to make sure my lighter and smokes are still there. Yep! Thanks, Andy. Slipping through the silent house, I let myself out the front door and into the chilly air. Pacing back and forth across the front porch, I struggle to think of anything but my dad lying dead somewhere in the Florida swamp. Or of the spot on the sidewalk where Mommy lay. Or of Mommy's grave. Maybe a few minutes of kill time on the computer will help.

Back inside, I sit in the chair and touch the mouse. The computer screen springs to life. Funny, the Addisons always shut the computer off before turning in for the night. What's this? Oh yeah, that Bible Gateway page Luke was showing me.

In the darkness, I catch a movement at the top of the stairs leading to Luke's and Sara's rooms. Sara is sitting there. She gives me a slight nod, gets up, and goes into her room.

I get it. She wants me to read this. Okay. Psalm 31:1-5. "I run to you, God; I run for dear life. Don't let me down! Take me seriously this time! Get down on my level and listen, and please, no procrastination! Your granite cave a hiding place, your high cliff aerie a place of safety. You're my cave to hide in, my cliff to climb. Be my safe leader, be my true mountain guide. Free me from hidden traps; I want to hide in you. I've put my life in your hands. You won't drop me, you'll never let me down."

I read it twice, letting the words sink in. Sara's right. I have nowhere else to turn. I need God. Right now, more than ever. God won't drop me or let me down. I think about our future. Will He always take care of Jose and me, even if it turns out Poppy is dead? Or if the investigation is a dead end? Shaking my head, I take a deep breath, letting it out slowly. Maybe. Please God. Closing down the computer, I climb the stairs to our room.

As I get into bed, Jose stirs next to me. "You smell just like Dee." He rolls over, facing away from me.

I press my hand over my lips as if to block the smell, biting into my palm. Squeezing my eyes shut, I back off to the other side of the bed.

It's true. Each night, Big Dee drank and smoked his troubles away until he passed out. What kind of example am I setting for the one person who means the most to me in the world?

34

A Day Off School

Friday, I wake to Danny's knock at 5:30 with the report that double overhead waves are going off right now two hours north of Boca. Since it's a no-school day, Jose asked to ride along to see what surfing upcoast was all about. Danny and Luke promised him a fun day of surf lessons. I look out the window as they ride off into the early morning.

In the kitchen, Sara pokes around the cupboards for breakfast. "Cereal and blueberries?" She glances at me, rubbing her eyes.

"Sure, sounds good."

"Here you go." She pushes over a large bowl of cereal and fruit. Her phone vibrates on the counter. She reads the text from Piper out loud. "Hey, did you still want to go shopping? How about shopping in Miami? Justin just texted me and I thought we could go hang out in Hialeah today. He's coming up for the weekend to surf. Danny invited him to stay at his house." Sara looks up at me. "Do you want to go to Hialeah?"

Surprised, I nod. This is too easy, will take me right where I want to be. But I can't go anyplace where I might run into Justin's stepfather. I made a promise to Chief yesterday. Still... "Hey, do you think we could drive over to the cemetery again? I want to see if anyone has been visiting Mommy's grave. Maybe they keep records. We had to sign in yesterday, right?"

"Yes! Maybe we can help Chief." Sara texts Piper to come pick us up at 9:00. I don't tell Sara I also promised Chief that I'd let him know if I was leaving Boca or seeing Justin. I'm only going shopping with friends and to visit my mom's grave. What bad thing could happen? It's a day off school, and I could use some freedom.

Sara and Piper sit in the front seat, chattering away about girl stuff, while I consider the possibilities of this day. After picking up Justin, we could go check in at the cemetery. Maybe while the girls are shopping, we'll borrow Piper's car and ride around my old neighborhood. Does Justin have his driver's license? Where is Justin's stepfather today? If Detective Andecker is involved in a drug shipment from Colombia, then Espinoza will be in Miami. Should I tell Justin what's happening? It's plain to see that there's no great love between them.

My ears perk up when I hear Piper's GPS lead us straight to 10410 NW 122nd Street in Hialeah. It seems like a lifetime ago that Andy and I drove to this same address. So much has happened since.

Justin comes out of the house carrying his backpack and surfboard. His mother is following close behind. "Hey Mom, these are my friends from Boca, Piper, Sara and Pedro." We get out to meet Mrs. Espinoza. Justin's mom is very short and is wearing a blue and gold Mother of Mary pin on the collar of her housedress.

Mrs. Espinoza smiles. "Would you like to come inside? I'm making empanadas.".

"No, Mom. We're going shopping and then back to Boca. Remember, I told you I'm staying at my friend Danny's house for the weekend? Big waves up there." Justin is trying to fit his board into Piper's small car. Mrs. Espinoza says something in a low voice, to which Justin replies, "Even if Craig is staying in Miami this weekend, I'll be fine. These are my friends, Mom."

"Why don't we come back and pick up your surfboard on the way to Boca?" Piper looks at Justin. "That will give you guys more room in the back while we drive to the mall and the cemetery."

"Cemetery?" Mrs. Espinoza asks. "You're going to a cemetery? Why?"

"My mother was killed in an auto accident," I say.

"Oh! So very sad." She reaches over and puts her arms around me. "When you come back for Justin's surfboard, I'll have empanadas made for you." She pats my cheek, smiling at us. "Many."

"Wow! That would be awesome." I rub my stomach. "I haven't had real, homecooked empanadas in a long, long time, Mrs. Espinoza."

"Okay, Mom. See you later," Justin says. It's easy to see he's trying to make his getaway. He's lucky to have a mom to come home to, one who cooks for him.

"What time?" she asks. Justin shrugs, glancing at Piper.

"Three? Four?" Justin asks.

"Let's say 4:00." Piper smiles at Mrs. Espinoza. "It has been a while since a mom made me a homecooked meal, too. I wouldn't miss it!"

"Don't encourage her." Justin laughs. "She'll cook up a banquet." Turning to his mother, he says, "Ma, solo empanadas. Si?"

With a sly smile, she picks up his surfboard and walks back to the house. "Claro, claro." She waves his comment away.

Inside the car, Justin says, "Thanks for coming to rescue me. I love my mom and all, but Hialeah is far, far from the ocean. The kids in this neighborhood would rather smoke dope than surf. Our street is changing. A lot of new people are moving in. Sara, thanks for introducing yourself the other night. It's good to have new friends."

"Yeah, especially when life is shifting all around you, and you have no control over it." Piper sounds sad as she looks over at Justin. "Has anybody bought your house yet? We have a For Sale sign on our lawn, too. That's why my mom and I live in an apartment."

"There is an offer on our house. If the sale goes through, we'll have to leave in about a month and a half, sometime around Christmas, I guess." Justin gazes out the window, sounding hesitant to talk about his future. I understand firsthand. He looks at Piper. "So, what's the plan now that you guys are here in Miami?"

"Shopping, shopping, and shopping! I hear Dadeland Mall is the place to power shop in South Miami," Piper declares, and Sara nods, smiling broadly.

"At some point, I need to go to Ave Maria Cemetery in west Kendall to visit my mother's grave."

"Let's go shopping, eat lunch at the food court, and then drive out to the cemetery," Sara suggests.

"Sounds like a plan. I'll show you the sights of The Magic City if we have time. It's a cool place if you know where to go," Justin offers as Piper pulls into traffic on the Palmetto Freeway.

35

Miami

Justin and I rest on a bench outside a trendy clothing store at the Dadeland Mall. I bite into an authentic Cuban sandwich wrapped in waxed paper. Mmm, just the right blend of ham, cheese, pickle, and mustard. I have to learn how to make these at home ... at the Addisons'. Leaning back, I tap my heel to the Latin dance music in the background. Families walk by, laughing, speaking rapidly in Spanish. Dark-haired girls wearing expensive perfume walk by, too, checking us out. They're there to be seen. Arroz con leche is strong in the air, and I turn my head to follow the smell. Yes, it feels good to be home.

"My mom used to make the best rice pudding. I miss her cooking the most. Only a mom knows what your favorite food is—and how to make it," I say.

"Let's go get some. The girls won't miss us. The food court is right over there." Justin points.

We lapse into speaking Spanish, comparing our lives while growing up in Hialeah. It's like Justin and I have been friends forever—even if he's Craig Espinoza's son. That's the way it is with us Cubans. We're a tight-knit community. If there's a bonding, it's fast and complete. The trust is here. I know Justin feels it, too. It's as if we've been friends all our lives. In fact, we went to the same middle school and even had a few friends in common.

Justin is curious about my parents. I struggle. How much do I reveal about the way our lives are bound? Justin will soon learn everything as the truth unravels. I don't want my new friend to feel like he's being used, or worse yet, betrayed, by me. But I'd be breaking my word to Chief and Andy if I breathe a word about the case. Andy! He can help.

I reach for my phone and text: Hey, where are you? Sara, Justin, Piper, and I are at the Dadeland Mall.

Andy messages back: I'm here, too. Looking for new seat covers for my Jeep. Head over to the Nascar store.

I stand up and look around. "Hey, Justin, where's the Nascar store? Danny's brother, Andy, is there shopping."

"Around that bend." Justin points. "Are you going now?" He stands up, looking inside the store in front of us. Sara and Piper disappeared into it a while ago. "I see Piper. It looks like she's going into the changeroom. How can that be fun?"

I laugh, shaking my head. "Don't know. Do you mind if I leave you for a few? When the girls finish up, come find us in the Nascar store."

"Sure. People watching at the mall is one of my favorite things to do."

Andy's at the checkout, paying for the seat covers. He holds them up. "Check these out. They'll be the coolest thing about my old Jeep. I left the top down last night, and it poured rain on my seats." He grins, pointing to the wet seat of his khaki shorts. "These new covers are waterproof! Good to see you, buddy. What are you doing in South Miami? You look super serious."

"Well, yeah. Come on outside so we can talk." I lead the way into the mall, talking as we walk. "So, Sara, Piper, and Justin Espinoza are here shopping today."

"Justin Espinoza!" Andy stops, staring at me.

"Yeah, long story. Sara's friend Piper and Justin are turning into good friends. We're all becoming good friends with Justin. He's a legit dude, surfer, and a good time all round. You might say that in the past week, we've become his Boca friends."

Andy nods slowly, his eyebrows knit together.

"So, last minute, Justin invited Piper down to Miami for the day. No school. Piper invited Sara and me. Seems Danny suggested Justin stay at your parents' house for the weekend to surf. So, here we are. We picked Justin up at his house, met his mom and all. We're going back there for some homemade empanadas around 4:00, and then heading back to Boca with Justin. After Sara and Piper buy everything in this mall. And after we go visit my mom's grave this afternoon." Noting the look of alarm on Andy's face, I stop speaking.

"Whoa. Whoa! This is way out-of-control, Pedro. Is Chief aware you guys are down here?"

"No. I only wanted to tag along, hoping to go to the cemetery. But Andy, knowing how things are going and how Justin is one of us now, soon he'll know about his dad and my mom and the hit and run. What then? I don't need him to feel betrayed, like I'm using him. He's going through enough stuff already. Should I tell him something? I started this whole situation by identifying Justin at the swim meet. That's why I texted you."

Repeating my thoughts to Andy causes me to realize how things could get real messed up if I don't watch out. He sinks onto a bench outside the store, silent. I recognize too late that our spur-of-the-moment Miami road trip could complicate matters and possibly jeopardize the case.

"Pedro, I can't give you permission to tell anybody the details of an open police investigation. Danny told me what a great guy Justin is—and how attached you're all becoming. There's more at risk here than a friendship, including your father's safety. If you're meant to be great friends, Justin will have to decide that when the time comes to tell him the full truth. After this case is closed. Are we clear on that?"

"Yes. I guess I just needed to hear it out loud." I sit next to him, looking down at my feet. He's right. I was way out of bounds with all of this.

36

Andy

"Okay, give me a minute to think this through." Andy stares into the distance for a few minutes. "Do you think Justin, Piper, and Sara would mind hanging here at the mall while I take you over to the cemetery? My Jeep seats are soaked, but these may help a bit." He holds up his new seat covers.

"Here they come. I'll ask." I breathe a sigh of relief. Andy's direction is what I need right now. Without thinking of the big picture, I stepped into a deep hole. I'm in way over my head. I don't even want to think about Chief right now.

"Hey, Andy! What are you doing here?" Sara smiles. "This is Justin and Piper. Hey, guys, meet Danny's big brother, Andy. He lives down here. Goes to UM."

"Good to meet you guys," Andy says. "Hey, I was just telling Pedro that if you wanted to stick around here, shop and hang out, I could drive him out to the cemetery. What do you think?"

"Sure." Piper smiles up at Justin, who nods.

"I want to go to the cemetery with you guys. I just bought daisies to put on Mrs. Ramirez's grave." Sara holds up a bouquet.

"Okay, that works. Where should we meet when we're all done?" Andy asks.

"We can meet at my house around 4:00. But come hungry," Justin says.

Soon, we're cruising west on Kendall toward the cemetery. Andy pulls into the parking lot. It's only been twenty-four hours, and my hopes have done a one-eighty. I need to stay positive about Poppy being alive. It's just a matter of time till Chief and Andy locate him. Sara scoops up her daisies, and we walk over to the small building. The same cheery lady is there to sign us in.

"Just sign in here." She smiles up at me.

"Thank you, ma'am. I was wondering if you keep a record of people who've visited my mother's grave. I only found out yesterday, after a year and a half, that she's buried here. I need to know who else has been to visit her."

"Well! That is a highly unusual request. I'm not supposed to give out that information."

"Please." My voice drops to a whisper. "My mother and father were reported to have been killed in a hit and run accident. I finally found her grave, but no grave for my father. He might still be alive." A tear falls down my cheek, landing on her ledger, smearing the ink. She stares at it, then looks up at me.

"My goodness, yes! That story was in the papers. So tragic!" She begins typing on her computer. "Everybody's at lunch. So, let me peek… Ah, yes, here we go. A Marcos Franks has been here. It looks like he visits twice a week. Every Tuesday and Saturday." She looks up, eyes sparkling, a wide grin spreading across her face. "Oh yes, I recall him! He's tall, with black hair. He's middle-aged and wears a chauffeur's uniform. Very handsome. He arrives in the morning, around 11:30. Drives a brown and tan Rolls Royce. A nice man. Does that sound like your father?"

"Not at all, but thank you for your kindness, ma'am," Andy says before I can respond. "Has there been anyone else?"

She looks back at the screen. "Let me see. A sizable group of people arrived yesterday. That was you." She smiles at me. Then a Mr. Espinoza came later in the afternoon. I recall him. Quite rude. Demanded to learn the names of everyone in your memorial group. Like I said, we don't release that information." Glancing at Andy, I can see he's as surprised as I am. Is it because Espinoza came too? I raise my eyebrows slightly, and he gives a small nod. Not good.

"Thank you so much, ma'am," I say. "I feel better knowing someone's been visiting my mother's grave."

"You are so welcome, son." Smiling again, she buzzes us out. Andy slings his arm around my shoulders, and Sara puts her arm around my waist. We walk to Mommy's grave.

"Are you okay?" Andy asks. I nod, swallowing hard and smiling at the same time. "Chief needs to know this. I'll be in the Jeep when you finish." He turns and heads to the parking lot, phone to his ear.

"Wow, Sara! Poppy is alive. He was here on Tuesday. Probably standing in this exact spot. I know right where to find him tomorrow morning at 11:30. God surely hears prayers."

"Pedro, have you been praying for that? I'd always assumed your dad was in heaven."

"Yeah, I never truly felt it ... felt it right here." I tap my chest. "I never really thought that he'd passed. With my mom, it seemed final. Never with Poppy. Maybe because they never found his cross, wedding ring, or anything he had on him the day he died. I had my mom's cross and earring but nothing from my dad. It made me crazy. I wanted to hope, but it seemed so impossible, especially during the darkest days, when traveling with the circus."

Sara takes my hand and prays, "Heavenly Father, through Jesus we come to You in thanksgiving for leading us straight to Pedro's father. You are an amazing and loving Father, full of grace. We joyously praise Your Holy name. Please keep Frank Ramirez and his two sons safely in the palm of Your hand until they are brought together once again. Thank you, Jesus. Amen."

She squeezes my hand, then we sprinkle the daisies on the grass over Mommy's grave. Bending down, I arrange the yellow flowers to spell MOM in the green grass.

"Wait!" Sara calls out as she steps back, searching in her bag. Pulling out her camera, she takes a few photos of me finishing the second M. It's a special moment. "Okay, now look up... Good one. Now you and me, okay?" She holds the camera high over our heads so we can get the daisies in the background. "That's my favorite!" She swipes across the images she took, stopping at the one of us.

"See you tomorrow, Mommy. And Poppy!" I say as we walk back to the Jeep. "I should call Jose. I want to see his face when I tell him."

"This is face-to-face news. Too big for the phone. Let's skip the sightseeing in Miami and drive straight back to Boca."

"Sounds good. And Sara…" I turn to her. "We need to keep quiet about this in front of Piper and Justin. Andy said it's for our safety. And now my dad's, too. Thank you, Jesus!" I shout to the sky. "This is so awesome!"

"I can't wait to see the look on everyone's face when you tell them. Luke and Danny should be back from their surf run by the time we get home."

37

Crash with the Past

I text Justin: DUDE, LET'S MEET BACK AT YOUR HOUSE. I NEED TO GET BACK TO BOCA SOONER THAN EXPECTED.

Justin: BE THERE IN HALF AN HOUR.

Andy pulls up to the house just as Piper and Justin come around the corner. She parks at the curb in front of Justin's house.

Sara hops out of the Jeep and runs over to Piper's car. "What did you guys buy? Show me, show me!"

"These girls are really passionate about their shopping." Andy laughs as we follow her.

Justin gets out and Sara gets in. "Air, air. I need some air. These girls are like madwomen." He reaches into the back seat. "Look! Piper bought me a rain stick. I've always wanted one." He tips the long, hollowed out tree limb so we can listen to the "rain sound," then lays it back on the seat. We watch the frenzy inside Piper's car as the girls sift through mounds of tissue paper. Giggling, Piper holds up a pair of red running shoes to show Sara.

Looking up, I wave at Justin's mom, who is standing on the front porch. Smiling, she waves back. She also waves at someone across the street. A man in a baseball cap rests in the shade on the front porch of a rundown house. Mrs. Espinoza joins Justin, Andy, and me.

Andy turns to her. "Hi, Mrs. Espinoza. My name is Andy Wainwright. Pedro told me you were making homemade empanadas, so I tagged along. Something smells fantastic! I hope you don't mind if I bust in on your meal."

"No, never. I make a lot. I even make for my friend over there." She nods at the man across the street. "Nobody know his name. We call him Buddy because he is a friend to anyone who needs one. Buddy is always here to listen to problems and fix things when they break in the house. Funny thing..." She lowers her voice. "He pulls a little pad of paper out of that dirty brown jacket and writes in it every day. Then he walks up the street and disappears into the dark. Bye-bye. No see him until next afternoon. Nobody knows where he sleep or why he no sleep in that house. The landlord—she my friend—say Buddy pays his rent the first of every week. So, no problem. He likes my cooking. Who's hungry? Come, come!"

Then I overhear her mutter to Justin, "Oh no, here come trouble."

Glancing up, I see the Crown Vic glide around the corner, heading straight at me. For a split second, my eyes meet Espinoza's. Leaning into Sara's open front seat window, I try to hide my face, even though I know it's too late. He recognized me for sure. Sara glances past me, picking up on the danger as Piper chatters on, unaware.

Out of the corner of my eye, I see Craig Espinoza bolt out of his car and stalk over to me. Grabbing the back of my jacket collar, he jerks me around to face him. "I know who you are." He snarls. "What are you doing hanging around my son?" In a flash, Espinoza opens the backseat door of Piper's car and slides in, wrestling me inside with him.

I open my mouth to shout but close it tightly as he pulls a black handgun out of his jacket with his free hand. "Shut up! We're going for a ride. Now! Start the car!" he yells at a wide-eyed Piper. He's waving a sinister-looking revolver between me and the girls in the front seat. Piper screams and starts the car.

Suddenly Buddy appears, an even bigger gun in his hand. I hear the familiar voice. "Get your blood-stained hands off my son."

"Poppy!" I stare into my father's face. Buddy is Poppy?

Espinoza looks as if he's seen a ghost. He jabs his gun into the back of Piper's neck and screams, "Go!" The circle of cold metal forming a white mark on her neck sends a chill through me. I shiver as Piper steps on the gas. The car jerks forward.

"Poppy!" I shriek. Piper's car takes off up the short street, tires squealing through the intersection as she turns the corner. I watch through the rear window as my dad stands in the street, tapping on his phone. Andy is doing the same.

"Shut your mouth, boy! Pedro, you've turned out to be a big thorn in my side. You're never going to see your poppy again. Never!" He pushes the gun harder into Piper's neck. "Turn right to get on the freeway, Blondie. Yeah, that way. Now step on it! Go as fast as you can." Espinoza's voice is low and threatening as he speaks into Piper's ear. Sara turns to look at me. I know that look. She's ticked off! Not now, Sara.

I'm still struggling to get my wits about me. Too much is happening too fast. Poppy is living on 122nd Street! Of course he would be there, watching, waiting. This man took Mommy from us. And today I'm finally face to face with the one person I've fantasized about killing. Blood is rushing in my ears. My heart is beating so loudly I bet Espinoza can hear it. I need to clear my mind ... now!

My fists clench and unclench, but other than that, my body is paralyzed. Big Dee took me to the range several times, showed me how to shoot his gun. This black weapon, only inches away, is powerful and deadly. Whoa! Now he's pointing it at me! His eyes are filled with hate. Is it possible he hates me more than I hate him? Best not to get him madder than he is, although I'd like to—

"What would you like to do to me, Pedro?"

Is this madman reading my thoughts? "I'd like to crush your face and brains in, the way you smashed my mother's in when you slaughtered her with your car," I spit out at him, venom in my voice.

Espinoza laughs ... a maniacal sound. "Oh, you would, would you? Never gonna happen. You're going down. All of you. Today. I got plans for you, Ramirez, and your lovely little lady friends. Like I said, you've been a thorn in my side long enough. The big boss's eyes will light up as I describe, in detail, how I offed the three of you. He might even throw a cash bonus my way!" He laughs again.

Turning, Sara gives me a warning glance, grounding me at once. The danger this unhinged man poses is a deadly threat. We're speeding south on the Palmetto Expressway. To where? The Everglades? Floaters are found there all the time. Is Sara trying to get my attention? What's she doing? Stay focused. Why does she keep patting her ear with four fingers? What is she trying to say?

Ah ... my phone! Four? I don't know. I sit back in my seat and put my hand in my pocket, gradually pulling out my phone. Good! Espinoza is leaning forward between the two front seats... Doesn't see. Quickly, I slide my phone under the fabric of my shorts so it rests on my leg. I lean forward, struggling to understand Sara.

Again, she puts four fingers up to her ear, then rubs her neck. Thank goodness Espinoza is busy giving poor Piper driving instructions. In a last act of desperation, Sara stops rubbing for a moment, flips her hand palm side out and wiggles all four fingers at me.

Four... Sara helped me set up my phone the other day, and we put Andy's number on speed dial. Number four. Now Sara is holding up one finger, playing with her earring. My cue to wait for her next move? I'm glad someone in this car is thinking instead of just reacting—like me. I could learn a lot from this girl.

Sara declares, "'*Your enemies will be clothed in shame, and the tents of the wicked will be no more.*' An orange jumpsuit will suit you, Espinoza. Is that the color of shame in the Dade County prison system?"

Espinoza freezes for a second, then leans in and rubs his gun against Sara's neck. "Quoting Job ain't gonna help you now, little lady. You don't intimidate me with your God. Your threats are just words." She screams. I take that moment to press down on the number four on my phone.

Connected! I pray Andy and Poppy are still together so they can listen. Even get Chief to track us with the GPS somehow. I run my finger around the side of the phone, setting it to silent.

"Come on, girl. Drive this thing faster. You drive like a granny," Espinoza growls.

Piper is sobbing. "I don't even know where we're going. This is the fastest I've ever driven in my life. There's so much traffic! I'm scared!"

"Piper, stop crying," Sara says. "Where are we going, gunman? Key West?" I freeze. Sara is fearless. Will she go too far? Will Espinoza hurt her? I love this crazy girl as a sister and don't want anything ugly to happen to her because of me.

"I'll show you a gunman!" My skin crawls as I see, then hear, the distinct sound of Espinoza knocking Sara on the side of the head with his gun.

38

Undercover Angels

P iper screams, "Sara, be quiet! He'll knock you out!"

"I just asked where we're going."

"Take the next exit to the Dolphin Expressway," Espinoza tells Piper. Turning back to Sara, he growls, "So, what have we here? A fearless little lady? Before this night is over, you'll be squealing for your mama. And there won't be anybody to hear you except hungry gators. And from what I've seen, alligators are hungry all the time. They think people are tasty. They don't like their bones, though. Your bones'll be drifting out with the tide. The Gulf Stream current'll pick them up and poof! As if you disappeared into thin air. Yours won't be the first body I've disposed of that way. Yep, there's lots of ways to make someone disappear."

"Like you killed Isabella Ramirez?" Sara eggs him on.

"Shut up about her! Everything was fine until you dumb kids stuck your noses into my business. And my family's business. You don't mess with Justin!"

"Yeah, well, you had no problem messing with Pedro and Jose's family. Who drove the blue BMW? You or Andecker? I still can't figure that one out."

"I said, 'Shut up.' Or I'll roll you out of the car right here, going eighty miles an hour. Faster, Blondie!"

"It was stupid to kill Mrs. Ramirez and not Frank. Just like it's stupid to make Piper drive eighty miles an hour in Miami rush hour traffic while you're waving that gun around." *Why is Sara trying to get him so riled up? Is she trying to get him to confess? She could get hurt. But, on second thought, he sounds angry enough that he might even fall for it. Good call, sis. I got you covered. The phone line is still open. I pray Andy can hear all of this, but I wish the screen didn't glow so brightly.*

Again, Espinoza growls, making that threatening sound in his throat. "Okay, okay! Slow down, Blondie. Watch who you're calling stupid." This time, Sara doesn't squeal as Espinoza rubs the gun on her neck.

"Sara, stop. Please!" Piper groans.

"Sorry. I meant *dumb.* Yeah, dumb move to kill the mother and not the father." Sara won't leave it alone.

"I'm not dumb or stupid!" he yells. "The Ramirez parents were walking close together, holding hands. I had them both in my sights. Frank saw us at the last second. Andecker was riding in the car with me and took a shot at Frank, but he escaped. I was sure he was dead. That is, until he showed up today. There! Are you happy? Cause you're going to take that info to a watery grave. Tonight!"

"But I'll deliver you on that doomsday. You won't be handed over to those men whom you have good reason to fear. Yes, I'll certainly save you. You won't be killed. You'll walk out of there safe and sound because you trusted me. God's Decree." I smile, hearing Sara's confidence as she quotes God's words again. *Remembering Big Dee's downfall, I already know God will deliver us from this danger.*

"Yeah, yeah. Your precious Bible again. Jeremiah thirty-nine, to be more exact. My mama taught me well. Don't believe it. My gun is mightier than your God." He peers down and sees my phone lit up inside my shorts leg. "What's this?" Before I can move, Espinoza snatches my phone and flings it out the window. Then he whacks me on the side of the head with his gun.

Stunned, I slump back into the door. Everything is happening in slow motion. *What's this long, hard thing under my arm? Touching it with my fingers, I recognize it as Justin's rain stick. Not the baseball bat I'd fantasized about, but it will do. I grip it tightly. The car is slowing. Why? Where is this peaceful feeling coming from? I've done all I can. Jesus, please rescue us. We're in Your hands. I struggled to keep my eyes open,* to keep from going under, blackness clouding the edges of my vision. The car is hardly moving. Why?

I open my eyes. A row of tollbooths lies ahead, long lines at each booth. Bright red brake lights appear and disappear in the early evening twilight. Has Espinoza been too busy bashing me on the head with his gun to pay attention to traffic? We stop, trapped in a parking lot of cars.

"Get over to the TollPass lane!" Espinoza points to the express lane.

"I don't have a TollPass," Piper wails. "My mother will kill me if I get a ticket. She doesn't even know I'm in Miami!"

"Haven't you heard a word I've said, Blondie? I'm gonna kill you first," Espinoza growls in her ear. "Put the car in park. I'll drive!" He shoves the gun into his belt and opens the back door, turning his back to me while getting out of the car. Wrong move, dude!

I jam my shoe in the middle of Espinoza's back and shove with all my might. Unbalanced, he face-plants onto the hot pavement. I kick him again, this time with both feet. I get out of the car and stand over him. With both hands wrapped around Justin's rain stick, I pummel the man I've despised for so long. Harder. I need to hit him harder. And harder. And harder! "You're never going to hurt anyone I love again!" I scream at Espinoza, who struggles beneath me.

Sara comes around to where I'm battering Espinoza, grabbing the rain stick on my next upswing. Dazed, I look up at her, then at Espinoza, who is lying motionless on the asphalt.

"Pedro, it's over." She points to three men and two women in black jackets that read FBI running over to us ... surrounding us, guns drawn. "It's over," Sara repeats, letting go of the stick and pulling me away from Espinoza. I study the rain stick in my hand. What? How? Spent, I drop it on the pavement next to Espinoza.

I'm dazed, as if in another world. Everything is still happening in slow motion. Sara and the female agent walk me over to a black SUV. Piper is already inside. I turn for another look. Espinoza struggles to sit with the help of an agent. We get into the vehicle and watch through the tinted windows as he is handcuffed, then led to another SUV. Piper's car is flanked by black FBI vehicles and Miami-Dade police cars with flashing lights. Lots of them. I close my eyes. Were they following us the whole time? Undercover angels.

39

Thank You, Jesus

"Thank you, Jesus." I whisper. The girls are huddled close together. Piper leans over and gives me a questioning look. "I prayed for help, and He delivered. Right there in your car." Piper takes a deep breath and begins sobbing hysterically. Sara shakes like a leaf. Stunned and spent, I rest my head on the seat back, rubbing the bump on the side of my head.

We hug and hang on to each other the entire drive back to Justin's house. The reality of what would have happened if I hadn't made that phone call sinks in. I feel rotten for breaking my promise to Chief, realizing fully why he made me promise to stay put. Too late.

"Hey, hey. You're safe now. I'm Agent Hannah, and this is Agent Ella." The taller agent gives Sara and Piper each a cell phone. "Time to let your parents know you're okay. They need to hear it from you."

"Daddy?" Sara can barely speak. "It's Sara. And Pedro. You're on speaker... We're safe. I'm sorry I went to Miami today without telling you." In the background, Danny lets out his signature whoop, the one reserved for catching the best wave. Sara looks up at me, grinning.

"Honey! We were so worried," Mrs. Addison cries. "Please come home as soon as you can." On the other end, everybody begins talking at once. I give Sara a look of relief. Things are back to normal. Whatever that is. For now.

Hearing my brother's voice, I ask, "Jose? Do you know who I saw?"

"Poppy! Yes! Andy called me. Poppy and I got to talk! He sounds just the way he used to. We prayed for you guys."

"There was lots of praying going on. I can't wait for us all to be together. See you soon. I love you." A sob escapes as I recall how close I was to never seeing Jose, Poppy, my family, and friends again.

Agent Hannah gives the Addison's the details of how Sara, Piper, and the rest of us will be taken home. After she picks up Ania and Justin from their house, we will all arrive at the Addisons' in about two hours. I squeeze Sara's hand. That sounds so good.

But what about Poppy?

"Agent Hannah. Is my father, Frank Ramirez, still at Justin's house?"

40

Winners

Poppy is waiting on Ania's porch as we drive up. Bolting out of the SUV, I sprint up the porch steps. Poppy hugs me. He keeps hugging me as if he'll never let go. That's fine with me. My tears fall fast. Pulling away, he wipes my cheeks, laughs, and pulls me into another bear hug.

"You're here. You're here," I keep repeating. The security I was robbed of, as Poppy's oldest son, fills me. I'm complete again, an orphan no more.

"Yes. Tomorrow we will begin returning to our way of life, life as it was before this tragedy. Family life."

"Wait. Tomorrow?" I step back. "What about right now? Today! You need to come back to Boca. See Jose. Meet the Addisons. Tonight. Right, Poppy?"

"No, Pedro. Not tonight. I have work to wrap up in Miami. Come inside. I'll explain."

Inside Ania's small living room, Poppy and Agent Hannah sit me down, explaining why it's essential for Poppy to be in Miami tonight. No! I will *not* part with my father. I just found him. Not now! This doesn't make sense.

"Pedro, what you don't realize is that your father has been working with the FBI. Frank is the key to completing our drug sting. It's happening tonight." Agent Hannah glances out the window. What is she looking for? "Before it navigates into the Port of Miami, a cruise ship will drop hundreds of pounds of cocaine and heroin, disguised as garbage, into the ocean. Andecker is the local player of the Miami drug operation who will pick up the bags and motor them to Miguel Mora's house on Star Island."

Before I can object, Agent Hannah continues, "We need your father to sneak our twelve FBI agents in the back of his F-350 into Mora's compound to complete our end of the sting. We'll catch Mora and Andecker and save thousands of lives. This drug shipment is the largest in the history of the Miami DEA. This is confidential information. We're only sharing it with you because you found your father only hours ago. I understand your distress, but—"

"It's true, son." Poppy holds my gaze. He needs me to understand his role. I get it, but I still want him to come with me. "I've positioned myself as one of Mora's valued employees. He's the drug kingpin here in Miami. Everybody trusts me, from the guard at the gate onto Star Island to Mora himself. Mora will be especially jumpy tonight if he's heard the news of Espinoza's arrest."

Agent Hannah gives Poppy a warning look. What? Does she think he's telling me too much? We're family. This is all so confusing. I'm hearing his words but cannot watch Poppy walk out of my life right back into the middle of danger. Running my fingers through my hair and tucking it tightly behind my ears, I stare at the floor.

Poppy lifts my chin with his finger. "We've planned and finetuned this sting for the past seven months. I can't let these agents or your mother down. It's for Mommy, Pedro. I must do it for her. You understand, don't you?" He appeals to me in a low voice. Shaking my head, I look out the window. Just then, three black SUVs pull up. More FBI agents? No, this isn't happening!

"We have to be going," Detective Hannah says. "Now."

I grab my father's arm with both hands. "Poppy, no! Let someone else help the FBI. It's too risky. Everyone has guns, and they'll use them. We can't lose you. Not again. Jose and I need you!"

"Pedro, I promise you I'll return to you and Jose tomorrow morning. I want to get the man who ordered your mother killed and who shot me, too. Andecker." He spits the name out of his mouth.

"But we have evidence that Andecker was involved with Mommy's death. We have her earring and cross. The police in Hialeah know Andecker is a dirty cop. Tell him, Andy." I'm desperate, turning to Andy, who's been standing by the door.

"We do have solid evidence proving Espinoza is linked to your mother's accident. We don't have any concrete evidence against Andecker though," Andy says.

Agent Hannah walks toward the door. "Ramirez, we must leave. Now!" She means business.

He holds my face in his hands and stares into my eyes. "Son, I must do this. I need you to understand, Pedro. If you do, it'll make it easier for me." He pulls his baseball cap off and puts it on my head backwards. "Take care of this. I'll be back for it in the morning."

After a few long seconds, I nod and lock Poppy into a fierce hug, tears streaming down my face. "Okay. For Mommy."

"For Mommy," he repeats.

"I'll stay at my place until you return, Frank." Andy turns to me. "I'll bring your father up to Boca as soon as he's finished here, Pedro. Deal?"

"Deal." I swallow hard. This will be the longest night of my life.

Ania, who has been silent until now, gets up and shyly takes Poppy's hand. "I will pray for your safety, Buddy."

"Thank you, Ania. We'll share empanadas again. Soon. Do you understand what's happening here?" he asks.

"Yes. I know for a long time my husband and Andecker are bad people. Tonight, you catch them and put them in jail. Good. Justin and I can finally have a new life. Life without fear, fear, fear. Always fear! This is what I want, too." She puts her arm around her son's waist and hugs him.

"Justin?" Poppy asks.

"Craig's been my biggest worry for a long time. Watching my mom suffer his abuse, living in constant fear, has been hard. It will be great when that part of my life is over. We can have a normal life like everybody else. Every time I got into that BMW with Craig, we'd stop and sell drugs to someone. Sometimes to kids younger than me. It was so wrong." Justin looks at his mom, who looks sad and shakes her head. I see evidence of the pain they lived with every day.

There's a light tap at the door. Another FBI Agent says, "Ramirez, let's go."

"I've got to go. If I don't show up at Mora's place by 9:00, he'll get suspicious. I love you, Pedro! Hug Jose for me."

"Wait, Frank, give me your phone so I can get a picture of you two together," Sara says. Poppy and I stand close together with huge smiles on our faces as Sara photographs us, first on Poppy's phone, then with her own camera. Poppy looks at the picture, touches my face, and mouths a *thank you* to Sara. After one last hug, he slips out into the night. The rear hatch on his truck bed slams shut, the powerful engine coming to life.

A Bible sits on top of the piano. Ania opens it. "God says, '*No matter what happens, I'm with you and no one is going to be able to hurt you. You have no idea how many people I have on my side in this city.*' I will sleep well tonight, knowing Frank and the agents are safe." Putting her short arms around me, she whispers in my ear, "Believe it."

"Thank you Ania." Knowing she's right, peace floods me. I hug her back.

"Mrs. Espinoza, we've arranged for you and Justin to sleep at my parents' house in Boca tonight. Is that alright with you? We think it'll be safer if you both leave Miami," Andy says.

"I'll drive you all to Boca tonight. The sooner, the better. If that's okay with you, Mrs. Espinoza," Agent Ella says.

"Si, si. Justin, get packed. I will be just a few minutes. Agent Ella, please call me Ania." She hurries out of the living room, untying her apron and throwing it on the chair.

Justin calls after his mom, "I'm already packed, Mom. Remember? I was going to Boca for the weekend to hang with these guys. Hey, maybe you can finally come and watch me surf." He looks at me, smiling widely. "Craig's gone. Outta my life. What a relief!"

"Yep, it looks like we both won the lottery tonight, bro." I smile at my new friend.

41

Come Home to Us

The drive back to Boca is quiet. What a day! How Sara had the presence of mind to get a confession from Espinoza with a gun pointed at her head blows me away. It has to be her faith. Fearless faith. Will my faith ever be that fearless? Is the time of pain in my life over? What will it be like to wake up without the intense hate that's been my fuel?

Taking off Poppy's hat, I turn it around and gently put it back on with both hands, running my fingers over the NY embroidered on the front of the cap. The few minutes I had with him reminded me of the love I thought I'd lost forever, his love. What if he doesn't come back from this night? He's a key part of the plan to bring down the Miami drug ring. What if he gets hurt? Or killed?

I can't go there. I must remember God is with Poppy tonight. Fearless faith. When it fades, I'm back in that black, hopeless pit. I need more faith. Not booze or cigarettes. Not kill games. Those aren't the answer. Didn't work last time. But why is faith hard to hold on to? Why does it slip away so fast? Where does it go? If it's a choice—a decision, like Sara says—then Jesus, please help me always make that choice.

I touch Sara's arm. "Back in Piper's car, when you quoted the Bible to Espinoza, how did you do that? Trust God when you were scared?"

"Pedro, God hears us whenever we call out. I know if I declare His Word into our circumstances, that He's there with us."

I watch the night lights of Miami flicker past the window. The ca-thump, ca thump of the tires makes me think of a kind of prayer. Come home to us. Come home to us.

"All I can do now is pray for Poppy's safe return. God has answered so many prayers since I began praying again." I turn to Sara. "Yeah, God's been true to me. He gave me the instinct to lay blankets over Jose and I in the boxcar, and we survived the blast. Also, the arrest of Big Dee, the love and support of the church, my hand and foot surgeries, your family and home. School. Poppy. The list of blessings is endless." Sara squeezes my arm. Leaning my head back and closing my eyes, I relax into the soft leather seats.

My gut clenches, and my eyes pop wide open. What have I done to make God smile? Nothing. Less than nothing. An overwhelming sense of dismay fills me as a shot of adrenaline hits me inside. It's tough to breathe. I gotta tell someone about my drinking and gaming or I'll puke right here. Have I messed up beyond the forgiveness of my new family and friends? Of Poppy and Jose? Of God?

"Sara!" She looks at me, eyebrows lifted. "I have to confess a few secrets, but you can't hate me, okay?"

"Sure." Sara tilts her head sideways, pulling her hoodie back. "Why would I hate you, Pedro?"

"Wait until you find out what I've been doing. It's hard for me to explain to anybody—even you." Staring forward, I feel my chest tighten. I avoid facing her. Taking a deep breath, I whisper so only she can hear. "So..."

"Yeah?" She nudges me with her elbow to continue.

"When I was with the circus, Big Dee used to drink himself to sleep every night. If there was any rum left in the bottle after he passed out, I'd finish it off. It helped me forget Mommy and Poppy. Jose and I being homeless. Having to live off the grid in fear of the authorities. I was super lonesome. Couldn't fall asleep most nights. The rum helped me sleep and forget all that."

Sara sits up straighter and reaches over to hug me. "Yeah?"

"When we all started going to the UM football games in Miami, I'd make myself a drink of rum when no one was looking, pour some rum into my can of soda. No one suspected. One night, I took a full bottle of rum from the bar in the skybox and slipped it into my backpack. I stashed it in my bathroom and drank every time things started getting uncertain about the case. If I still couldn't sleep, I'd go downstairs and log onto the computer.

There are lots of violent games online. I was drinking and gaming every time I couldn't sleep. When gunning down the victims, I fantasized I was gunning down Espinoza and Andecker. It felt great, powerful. Revenge is addictive."

Sara nods. "I saw you gaming on the computer but didn't know what to do. You looked scary intense last night. I know this past week has been a roller coaster for you. You've had so much happening in your heart and head, Pedro. And you share so little."

"True. Trust is hard for me. We had to keep most of the investigation secret because it was ongoing police work. So. I finished the first bottle. I put it in a neighbor's recycle bin when I went out for a walk one night, swearing I'd never drink again." Turning, I let my breath out slowly, causing a circle of vapor on the window. I trace an X inside it with my finger. Do I have the courage to tell her about Tuesday?

"Umm..." She's waiting for more.

"Okay. Here's the worst part. If you never speak to me again, I'll understand."

"Stop, Pedro. Nothing you can do will wipe out my feelings for my new brother. Or new best friend. Or whatever you are now that your poppy is alive." She squeezes my arm again.

"He is alive. It's so incredible! I go to see if anyone is visiting Mommy's grave and find out Poppy is living across the street from Justin. And you, Sara! You were amazing in the car with that creep. You got the confession we needed to put him away for good. I will never forget that, Sara. Never."

"Okay, back to my list of secrets and horrible crimes. Tuesday, when we went to study at Danny's house, I stole another bottle of rum from his parents' liquor cabinet." There's a long silence. My face burning, I want to be anywhere but here. But I keep talking, as if a floodgate has opened. I need to get the rest of it out. My heart is beating so fast I might pass out.

I squeeze my eyes shut and say, "I stole from the man who operated on my hands. Who gave me my life back! It happened before I even knew what I was doing. I didn't plan it. I opened the cabinet door, and within a second, I picked up the closest bottle and dropped it into my backpack. You guys were out on the patio, and I was alone in the house. I hate myself." Exhausted, I hang my head.

"Where's the bottle now?"

"That's the worst part. I vowed to put it back as soon as I had the chance. Then, late last night, I started speculating that Andecker and Espinoza had already murdered Poppy. I got so crazed I opened that bottle and drank. I drank a lot. To take the hopelessness away. That's when I noticed you. Thanks, sis. That Bible verse was an arrow straight to my heart. The peace I got was real. But when I got back into bed, Jose rolled over and told me I stank like Big Dee. I felt like the worst big brother ever."

"Wow! I had no idea you were suffering so deeply."

42

Boca Home

Chapter 42 ~ Boca Home

"Now what?" I look out the window, my voice low and shaking.

"Confess your sins to each other, and pray for each other so that you can live together whole and healed," Sara whispers. "You've confessed to me, Pedro. Give me your hands. We'll pray. Jesus, please take our prayers to the Father. Pedro has sinned, and the fear of God is in him. He doesn't wish to be cut off from You because of his sins. Please show him Your grace and mercy as he repents and prays for Your forgiveness and strength." She squeezes my hand. I guess that means it's my turn.

With no idea what to say to God, my words come out slowly. "I've stolen ... from kind people. I've let my hatred and the need for revenge blind me to Your blessings. I'm so ashamed. Please, please, forgive me. I'll never do it again. Help me ... make it right. Please bring Poppy home safely from this night. Thank You. In Jesus's name. Amen."

"You took the first step back, Pedro. You're forgiven. The toughest part is over. The Lord will give us, and your father, uncommon strength to get through what's ahead. Remember Luke? He was in way over his head a month ago. He set his friend's house on fire!"

"Yeah, I know how he felt now that I have to face your parents, Danny's parents, my dad, and Jose. I might as well post it on Insta that I'm a thief, a drunk, and a kill junkie. I'm so ashamed."

"This is between Danny's parents and you. I agree it will be tough to face them, but God will help you through it, Pedro. Get them alone, return the bottle of rum, and confess your sin. Just like you did to me. They'll understand. They're doctors. They get it. No one else needs to know."

"You're right. Thanks for listening and praying. I'm better now that I know what to do. And that you're still my friend."

"I still have to explain to my parents why I went to Hialeah to see Piper's new boyfriend, who just happens to be Espinoza's son. You know the rest. Mom won't accept it, no matter what I say!" Sara looks at Piper in the seat behind us.

Piper groans. "Don't remind me. I'm toast, too. I predict the end of our friendship. At least the outside of school part of it." I shake my head. If today wasn't a bonding experience, I don't know what would qualify.

Sara digs in her purse. Finding her phone, she swipes to the photo of us standing by Mommy's grave decorated with daisies.

"That seems like a hundred years ago." I sigh loudly.

She swipes to the photo of Poppy and me. Wow! We look so much alike. Were the long ponytail and Yankees' cap part of Poppy's disguise? Sweeping my fingers across Poppy's hat, I decide to give it to Jose when we get home. While we were traveling thousands of miles north with Big Dee and the circus, Poppy sat on a porch across the street from Justin's house, waiting for the right moment to close in on those two criminals.

Familiar bumps shake the SUV as we turn into our driveway. The Addison's, Chief Howell, Jose, Luke, and Danny swarm around the SUV. After a bunch of hugs and introductions, we make our way into the house to retell the day's events. I plop Poppy's hat onto Jose's head. Breathing in, his eyes get big. Did he catch the scent of Poppy's aftershave, too? Danny grabs hold of Sara's hand and holds it tight. She smiles widely as he pulls her into a fierce hug. Her smile fades as soon as she looks at her mom. Yep, there will be a serious talk soon, and it won't be pretty when it happens. Agent Ella offers to take Piper home.

The night ends with Sara and me showing our pictures. Jose cries. We all pray for Poppy's and the FBI agent's safety. It's midnight before Danny, Ania, and Justin leave.

In bed, I pray again for forgiveness and the future of my family. After tonight, everything will change. Will Poppy want to move to Boca so we can live near Sara, Luke, the Wainwrights, our new church and schools? Maybe the Addison's or Pastor Thomas can help him find work. That would be perfect.

Peaceful for the first time in longer than I can recall, I drift in and out of sleep.

43

Red Letter Day

At 6:00 AM, I hear Danny's tap on the front door. Sara comes down the stairs as I open the front door. There stands Danny, Andy, and Poppy.

"Jose! Poppy's here!" Jose runs down the stairs, Poppy's hat on his head. I laugh, knowing Jose slept in it.

"Praise God!" Sara breathes, giving Poppy a huge smile. Poppy, Jose, and I hug, holding on to each other, laughing and crying. Sara, Danny, and Andy go into the kitchen. We follow them, everybody talking at once, asking Poppy about last night.

As Mrs. Addison picks up the coffeepot, Danny says, "Wait, Mrs. Addison! My parents sent us over here to get you guys. They're preparing a huge breakfast homecoming for Mr. Ramirez on the pool deck and want you all to come. Chief, too. My dad's making his famous breakfast burritos, quiche, bacon, sausage, French toast, the works. Ania is already in the kitchen, bossing everyone around. She's so funny. Had us laughing before we could even wake up all the way. Bring your bathing suits. I called Cheree, woke her up! She said she'll be there, too."

"That sounds fantastic." Mrs. Addison smiles, putting the coffeepot away. "We'll be ready in five minutes." She pulls Sara aside. "Don't make plans for today. We need to talk."

Danny and Andy walk over to invite the Howells to join us.

"Poppy, come see our room." Jose takes Poppy's arm. I run up the stairs ahead of them, needing to put Doc's bottle of rum in my backpack. Gonna do this. Today. It's a fresh starting point, and I need to do it with no demons in my closet, no regrets. My gut feels as if there are jumping beans going off inside.

"We're dressed and ready for food." Jose pats his belly as we meet on the front porch. He won't stop leaning on Poppy, as if Poppy might vanish. "I'm so happy for today. And now you can meet our new friends. Sara, will you bring your camera?"

"I'm one step ahead of you, little brother." Sara laughs, taking a photo of Jose and Poppy. "Okay, now the three of you guys." On our way out, Sara pulls me aside. "Are you going to return the bottle this morning?" I tap my backpack.

We caravan over to Danny's house in the early morning sunlight. A new day. A new life. I breathe in, smiling. Is this joy?

"Welcome!" Doc booms as we step into the Wainwright home. He goes straight for Sara. "Get over here, little lady! Big hero from what I hear. Let me look at you. I need to see for myself that you're alright." He crushes her in a bear hug as she struggles to nod and speak.

Letting go of Sara, Doc turns to swoop down on Jose and me. "This is a red-letter day, boys! Pedro, you're the spittin' image of your pa. Met Frank at dawn, when Andy brought him over after your dad helped clean up the Miami drug cartel. Frank! You have two fine boys here!" Ouch! If Doc had any idea...

Greeting the rest of the family, Doc motions towards the rear of the house. "Breakfast is on the deck. I hope you brought your appetites. I couldn't keep our little Ania here out of the kitchen. So, these burritos have a distinct Cubano flavor. This lovely lady is quite comfortable in an apron as you can see." Ania twirls around and curtsies, showing off her white apron and chef's hat. "Of course, I had to taste-test a burrito ahead of time to make sure they were good enough for company." He roars with laughter, giving Ania a big wink. "Has everyone met Ania and Justin Espinoza?"

The smell of bacon fills the deck as we surround the enormous table loaded with food. I heap my plate and sit next to Chief, realization rolling over me like a freight train about my broken promise to him. Too late to switch places now.

"Uh. Good morning. Chief." I swallow hard, heat creeping up the back of my neck.

"Pedro." He turns to me. Not smiling. "I'm giving you kids a full pass this one time and one time only. Don't push it."

"Yes sir. Thank you." It's all I can squeak out.

For the next hour, I help myself to seconds and thirds. Ania keeps bringing out freshly baked muffins and bread. After the plates are cleared away, Luke asks the question on my mind—and probably everyone else's. "Mr. Ramirez, we're so relieved you're here this morning. Where've you been for the past year and a half?"

We all turn to Poppy. He sips his coffee and stands. He's still the best-looking dad in the room. Always was! As he smiles, his face changes completely. His eyes light up, and his deep dimples appear on the sides of his mouth. As a kid, I'd stick my fingers into them and make him laugh. His perfect white teeth kinda give him the rugged look of a Cuban baseball all-star.

"Before I go into the past, including last night, I need to thank each of you for taking my sons into your hearts and homes. I cannot thank you enough. You cared for them in all the ways they'd been stripped of since they lost their mother and me that day. What happened to my family should never happen to any family. Luke, Sara, Danny, and Cheree, your friendship has restored my boys' faith in people. Mr. and Mrs. Addison, you saved their lives, hearts, and souls. Al and Dana, your kind medical treatments are helping Pedro and Jose live healthy, normal lives. Their dearly departed mother and I had been saving for these operations. To watch Pedro use his hands as a normal teenager melts my heart. Chief and Andy, your tireless probe into our deaths has reunited my family. And Ania, your kindness warmed my heart in the darkest times." He pauses, smiling at Ania as he wipes a tear from his cheek. "Yes, this is a red-letter day."

"The night Pedro and Jose's mother was killed I was also shot. From the angle of her neck, I immediately knew my wife was dead. I had to make split-second decisions, my boys being my priority. I dashed into the back alley because I knew these gangsters would stop at nothing to murder me, too. I knew too much, had learned too much about them and seen too much. Pedro and Jose were at risk. Bleeding, I found my way to Dr. Velez's door. He saved me. He dug the bullet out and bandaged my arm. After dark, we drove past my house, but you boys had already been taken. I watched the news that night. I was relieved the wrong people didn't have you and that you were protected.

"My plan was to lie low and let my body heal. I was in pain. In and out of consciousness. I actually hid out in my townhome. Nobody ever pays attention to a house where tragedy has struck. It was safe there. My single focus was to get my two boys and disappear from Miami forever. I was heartbroken when I saw on the news that two boys your ages had run away from a foster care home. I knew it was you and realized I'd never find you in this jungle of a city." Jose shifts closer to Poppy, who brings his arm around his shoulder. He looks down at Jose. "I hunted for you every day. I never stopped searching. I felt in my heart we'd find each other again."

Frank took a deep breath and continued, "As my strength returned, I formulated a plan. It required becoming indispensable to the man who employed Espinoza and Andecker, Juan Mora. I got my chauffeur's license, then watched the movement of Mora's household staff. My goal was to get as close to them as possible. His chauffeur regularly stopped at a small Cuban joint for a few beers at the end of his shift. I made it my business to become a regular at that bar. I became friendly with this man, Carlos."

"But Poppy, you don't drink beer," Jose says. "I remember."

"I'd drink snake venom if it helped me find you two and avenge Mommy's death." He pauses, smiling at us. "From there, it was simple. Carlos, Mora's chauffeur, and I had beers several days a week. When the day chauffer left, I got the job per his recommendation. For over a year, I listened and waited for the chance to take these guys down. Andecker and Espinoza weren't high enough in the chain of command to be summoned to Mora's house. My identity was safe even though I had to grow this." He grinned, flipping his long, thick ponytail forward.

"I would kill for magnificent hair like this." Ania sighs. Everybody laughs.

"You were a Godsend." Poppy beams at Ania. "As you know, I rented a room in the house across the street to monitor Espinoza. Ania would bring over plates of homemade Cuban food from time to time. Kindness from a stranger during long, lonely times is a very special thing." When Poppy smiles at Ania, his face softens.

"Hey, if I know this, I deliver a plate every day!" she declares, seeming to warm under his smile. Ania seems like she is one of those moms who isn't shy about speaking her mind, one who is fun to have around.

I glance at Justin, who is rolling his eyes and shaking his head. "Don't get her started."

"My life became routine, waiting for the day I could send every one of these guys to prison for good. I visited my Isabella's grave twice a week and promised her I'd find our boys. One day, I noticed I was being followed. After a time, I decided they were FBI. Black suits with ties, shiny wingtip shoes, and a dark SUV. The cemetery is far out in western Dade County. I approached them after visiting my Issa. We had a talk. I told them my story and soon became a participant in their drug sting. A valuable informant. I'd accessed places they hadn't—as a trusted staff insider in Mora's compound as well as living on the same street as Espinoza and Andecker."

"Then we stepped in and reopened the case," Andy says. "Were you guys aware of that? Did that complicate matters for you?"

"The FBI agents knew you were a student working with Chief Howell here, but they never told me. They didn't realize Pedro and Jose were my sons. They kept me focused on Mora, that the motherlode of all drug shipments was due to arrive last night."

"What happened last night, Poppy? Were you in danger?" I have to know.

"No, I wasn't in any danger. As planned, the twelve FBI agents hid in the enclosed bed of Mora's truck. I drove them past the security gate onto Star Island, right into Mora's compound. Once inside the garage, I opened the hatch of the truck. Like ninjas, they escaped into the night. My nighttime routine is to walk the perimeter of the estate and report directly to Mora that everything is secure. I did that at 10:00 PM as usual, then retired to my apartment over the garage."

"Then what?" I ask.

"Around 4:00 AM, I heard a boat motor up to the dock. From my upstairs window, I saw Mora in a white bathrobe, smoking one of his fat cigars. He carried a suitcase out onto the dock. Three men tied the boat up to the pilings. One of them was Andecker. They unloaded eleven stuffed garbage bags onto the dock. Mora, surrounded by four of his thugs, opened a penknife and slit into the top three bags. He stuck his little finger inside each and tasted it. It was a very relaxed transaction. I'd seen him do this a few other times, but never with that much contraband.

"Mora nodded, then passed the suitcase of cash to Andecker. Twelve FBI agents appeared out of nowhere and arrested every one of them. There wasn't much of a struggle. Mora must have known they had him. That was it. I don't believe anyone knows or suspects I was the one who brought the FBI into the compound. They could have easily arrived by water."

"Wow! Not like on TV at all!" Mr. A. says. "Then what?"

"Then Agent Hannah drove me to Andy's apartment. Andy brought me here. Here we are on this beautiful day, a day that I prayed for every morning and night. Mora paid me well. I continued to pay rent on our townhouse in Hialeah. Pedro, Jose, all your things are still in your rooms, untouched."

"My Marlins baseball card collection! Today is better than Christmas!" Jose exclaims.

"And we are safe from those bad people, too, Justin," Ania adds decisively. "Drugs are evil. Drugs are very, very bad. They break families. Look at our two families. Just because of drugs. Look at the children on the streets. So sad."

Mrs. Addison gets up and gives Ania, then Poppy, a hug. I remind myself to tell Poppy about the Rodriguez's and Dr. Velez's help. For now, I have some unavoidable business to take care of. I catch Sara's eye, and she gives me a small smile of encouragement.

44

Apology

"We need music!" Doc steps inside to turn on the outdoor speakers. I follow him in. Lord, give me the courage to confess to Doc.

"Sir, may I speak to you for a minute or two? Alone, I mean." Deep breath. Need complete sentences here. If I lived through yesterday, I can make it through this. I need Doc to know that I'm not a thief. How do I earn his trust after looting his liquor cabinet? He might figure I'll go into their bedroom next and steal their jewelry. He must believe I didn't plan this. That I'll never violate his trust again. I'm not a thief!

"Why, of course, son. Come into my study. What's on your mind?" The heavy wooden door clicks shut. No escape now.

"Uh. Hmm. I don't know where to start."

"Why, at the beginning of course. We have all day if you need it." Doc's blue eyes fix on me as he sits behind his desk. "Have a seat, Pedro."

"Okay. I used to drink sometimes at the circus, steal the owner's rum to fall asleep at night. Then, when you invited us to the football games in Miami, I slipped rum into my colas from the bar. It made matters more bearable as Andy and I investigated our cold case." I draw a deep breath. "I stole a bottle from the skybox in Miami, drank from it at night when things seemed hopeless. I took this from your home last Tuesday afternoon."

I hold out the stolen bottle of rum. "I didn't plan it. It just happened, and I'm so sorry. You've done so much for me, and I'm so ashamed. How can I make it up to you, Doc? What do I do now?" I stop, my cheeks burning. How could I have screwed this up so badly? My new life, new friends ... and here I am, doing sneaky, low-life stuff. I wouldn't blame Doc if he ordered me to leave his home.

Doc studies me for a long minute. "We are so human, aren't we?"

I stare at him. Whaaat? That's an odd reaction.

"I see this bottle's been opened."

"Yes, I meant to return it as soon as possible. After the memorial Thursday, I learned there was only one grave. My world went ink black, and I got desperate again. I drank to forget, to sleep. Not much though. Look here. Well, more than a sip." I point to the half-full bottle.

"Pedro, you're a brave young man. If the truth be told, I'd never have missed this one bottle from my cabinet. Let's make a deal. Today is a special day for you, your family, and for all of us who love you boys. Let's return to the celebration. Tomorrow, you, your father, and I will chat. We'll make a plan to defeat this potentially serious drinking problem. Thank you for telling me."

"Please don't judge me badly, Dr. Wainwright. I admire you so much." I'm close to tears.

"I don't judge you at all, Pedro. I want to support you. Once I had a problem with drinking. I experienced firsthand what you're going through."

"You?"

"Yes. In medical school. During my internship, a patient died while in my care. Just stopped breathing. I took it hard and started drinking during, as you put it so well, 'the ink black, desperate times.' Pedro, know this. We'll overcome this problem together. Now, get out there and enjoy your father's party!"

"Thank you so much, Doc. I'll call you tomorrow. Thank you." I can't express my gratitude enough.

The horror of my crime has lifted, and the dread of confessing to Doc has melted away. I walk out of Doc's office. The jumping beans in my stomach have vanished, replaced by a solid sense of belonging. I belong and am loved by these people—and Poppy. I take a deep breath as hope grows inside me. Is this what it's like to have God do His work in me? Is this the new life in Christ I prayed for with Sara? Sara! I need to talk to her. Now.

On my way out, I walk by the clown painting. It's crooked. I tap the right side to straighten it. I'll paint someday. Just not clowns. Never clowns. Yes, hope is good.

Outside, Sara and Danny are sitting at the end of the dock, feet in the water, feeding the fish. They look up as I hurry toward them.

45

Catching the Spirit

"Pedro. What's up?" Sara asks.

"I need to tell you something."

"Do you want me to take off?" Danny looks up, eyebrows raised. I do sound kinda serious, even for me.

"No, you should hear this, too, Danny." I sit next to them. "Sara, remember the prayer you prayed with Jose and I the day we first met?"

"Yes, the prayer of salvation."

"That was about a month ago, right?"

"Right. Just before school started." Sara smiles.

"In the past month, God has moved in my life." I point to the sky with my index finger. "Big time."

"Big time," Sara agrees, pointing up.

I grin at Danny, pointing up again. "It's a Latino thing. So, since then, I've been wrapped up in the highs and lows of finding Poppy. Mostly the lows. Definitely not seeing the full picture of how God has been working in me since we prayed that day. After speaking with Doc today, I sensed God's presence. I was light, almost dizzy. But not. I can't really describe it! Hopeful. More than hopeful. As if I'm complete. Without the booze, the cigarettes, the gaming, and everything else I was doing to make the blackness go away."

"What you're describing sounds like the presence of the Holy Spirit." Sara splashes water with her big toe.

"Yeah? Wow! I hope I never lose it."

"Pedro, you hear people talk about the fear of the Lord. God doesn't want us to fear Him in our daily life. Only to revere Him. Fear of the Lord is when you give in to temptation and trade the feeling you have right now for something that may feel necessary—or very attractive—at that moment. Like the rum, for example. You notice instantly when that light, hopeful sense of peace fades away. You're no longer in step with the Lord. To me, that's fear."

"I hear ya. I think. This is a lot. I need to think about this more." I have no words.

After a minute, Danny asks, "Will you pray the prayer of salvation with me?" Sara takes his hand, and we stand up on the dock, forming a circle. Sara says, "Danny, repeat after me... Pedro, join in if you wish. Right now, I confess Jesus as Lord of my life. With my heart, I believe that God the Father raised His Son, Jesus, from the dead. This very moment, I acknowledge that Jesus Christ is my Savior and, according to His Word, I am born again. Thank you, Jesus, for coming into my life. In Your name we pray. Amen."

Danny looks up as Sara continues, "We want to serve You, Lord Jesus. Starting now, we pray You help us hear Your voice. Lord Jesus, please change us so we may please You alone. Amen."

Yes. A red-letter day.

As we walk onto the pool deck, Luke asks, "Is Sara out on the dock saving souls again?"

"Yes. We prayed the prayer of salvation." Danny smiles.

"Praise God!" Ania cries, running over to hug him.

Poppy, then Mr. A, stand and come over to Danny, shaking his hand. "Welcome to the family of God, Danny." The rest follow and gather around Danny, taking turns hugging him.

"I don't know exactly what you're describing, son, but this sure feels like a special celebration." Doc says as he, Dana, and Andy join in.

"I'll tell you when I figure it out enough to put into words." Danny laughs.

Luke asks, "Danny, can I use your phone?" Danny digs into his pocket and hands Luke his phone. Luke raises his voice to be heard above the commotion. "I remember when they baptized me. It went something like this." He shoves Danny into the pool.

Dana says, "Oh no! Nobody is safe. Hand me your phones." She passes around a basket with a small, laminated sign: Pool Party Phones. I help her gather the rest of the cell phones.

"This is an excellent idea, Dana." Mrs. Addison raises her voice to be heard above the shouting and splashing. "I can't tell you how many phones have gone Davy Jones in our pool. It quickly ruins the mood of a pool party."

"Ha! Wait till they find out how much I charge to get these back." Dana laughs, putting the basket out of sight. "It's how we pay the mortgage around here!"

I'm about to somersault into the pool when I see Poppy answer his phone. He speaks quietly, then listens for a long time, his face showing no expression. Looks to be a serious conversation. Jose sits close to him, and I weave between the deck chairs, moving toward them. A gigantic grin spreads across Poppy's face. Speaking into his phone, he glances at me, then looks down at Jose.

"Yes. Thank you. I can't tell you where to send it right now. Obviously, I won't be living over Mora's garage any longer. Yes, I'll call. Thank you again, Agent Hannah." Poppy looks up, eyes wide.

"Poppy, what?" Jose asks.

"Miguel Mora has been on the US government's Most Wanted list for eleven years. There was a million-dollar bounty on his head. They're awarding it all to me." Poppy shakes his head, blinking rapidly, as if it's too good to be true.

"Hooray! Now we can move to Boca!" Jose bursts out. "We can stay in the same church and schools and live near our new friends." Everyone looks at Poppy.

"I guess that settles it." Poppy leans into Jose, fist bumping me. "Done."

"Justin and I have news, too," Ania says softly, glancing over at her son. "Agent Hannah tell me that Craig purchase a condo here in Boca. Paid for. Cash. She agree we are no longer safe at 122nd Street in Hialeah. So, Justin and I will move here until we make final decision. Agent Hannah says she will arrange this for us."

"Does Boca South need a fast freestyle swimmer to finish out the season?" Justin asks Luke.

"Yeah, bro! A pool initiation is in order." Luke nods to Danny and me. We lift Justin, carry him over to the pool, and throw him in.

Sara sits next to her mom. Uh, oh! Serious talk time. After a few minutes, Sara gets up, hugs Mrs. A., then performs one of her perfect dives into the deep end of the pool.

Surfacing next to us, she says, "Mom wasn't even mad. Just upset because I put myself in so much danger."

"I'm with her on that one," Danny agrees.

"I promised her I wouldn't do it again. I'm not grounded or anything."

"Promise me, too." Danny's words come out faster than normal, his face serious. "You don't know how it was. I was sitting at your kitchen table with Chief, Luke, Jose, and your parents. Then we heard you were in a car with an armed madman killer, speeding south on the Dolphin Expressway. Next, they told us Pedro's phone went dead." His shoulders shake. "God brought you back, and I don't want to lose you again, Sara. Ever." He puts his arm around her, pulling her in tight.

"Yeah, we thought we lost you, Cookie," Luke says. "We sat through a couple of long, terrible hours last night."

"I'm so sorry." Sara glances around. "I didn't realize... But we got Espinoza's confession. Right, Pedro?" she asks, rubbing the side of her head.

"That you did." I grin, wincing as I touch the knot next to my ear.

"You got off easy. Piper's grounded forever. She texted me earlier. So, what happened while you were in the car with Craig?" Justin asks.

I give Sara a guarded look. Not now. It's too close. All that rage. Spent on a highway in Miami. Fourteen short hours ago. I need time to process.

"That's not pool party talk," Sara says. "That's Costa Rican surf camp talk!"

The End

READ MORE OF LUKE, SARA, PEDRO, JOSE, DANNY AND FRIENDS!

VIRTUE FOR
VENOM
MEGY DAVIS
FAITH IN ACTION SERIES BOOK 3

WIPEOUT
MEGY DAVIS
FAITH IN ACTION SERIES BOOK 1

Preview Book Three: Virtue For Venom

PROLOGUE

When exactly did I, Sara Addison, change? A few weeks ago ... the exact day being Saturday, the day before the fall daylight savings time change. I woke, and keeping my eyes shut tight, rolled off my bed and landed on my knees. Hands in prayer position, I prayed the Lord's Prayer, like I do every morning. That will never change. "Our Father in heaven, holy is Your name..."

I rub my eyes open, blinking against the brilliant sun streaming in through my opaque, sky-blue curtains. Fresh air wafts in and tickles my nose, swirling in a cool breeze. The quiet whisper of the wind through the curtains sound like secrets, promises of the amazing things to come. Goosebumps rise on my arms and legs. Tiny hairs stand on end. My heart beats faster and faster.

Something is very different ... what is it? I stare at the ceiling, smiling. A silent shift begins inside of me. Uncontrolled, like a tectonic plate, my whole being slips and shifts. Sudden, and fresh wants, needs, desires, and passions rearrange themselves inside me. Powerful and intense, each fights for first place! These hurricane-force winds of change, so intense ... rapid whirling thoughts disappearing before fully forming.

I take a deep breath, saying yes to this thrilling moment! My world had tilted like a pinball machine, lights flashing and bells ringing, bouncing me between the bumpers of endless possibility. I grin at the chaos unfolding in me, certain that nothing will ever be the same again. That is just fine with me! Outside, a breeze blows the dead leaves from the lawn, across the sidewalk.

Inside, my heart hammering, I'm wide awake. Rolling back onto my bed, I bury myself inside my soft, down comforter and laugh out loud. Life is good. So, so good! Yes, it's time to live ... to do me! Do life on my own terms. It's time to step outside the box for a while ... explore where these amazing feelings take me.

Reaching over, I feel for my phone on the nightstand. First up, a triple heart text to Danny Wainwright ... the guy who makes me giddy inside.

I can pin down to the second, the main event that created this earthquake inside me. Danny's kiss ... when I discovered that saying 'yes' to life opens new and exciting doors. And some nightmarish ones!

Get your copy now, stay up all night reading!
https://www.megydavis.com/
Email me at: megydavis@megydavis.com
Insta: megydavis_ author_photographer
Threads: @megydavis_ author_photographer@threads.net
https://www.Facebook.com/SaltOfLifeFiction

About the Author:

I am a Christian, a free spirit, and a grandmother to anyone who needs one. I have a huge heart for teens and young adults. I pray my stories inspire young people to get to know the Lord by getting to know what He has promised—and that He delivers.

My background includes a lifetime as a professional photographer, business owner in the insurance industry, teaching ESL in Ft Lauderdale, and volunteering as an English language teacher in Spain, Italy, and Costa Rica. I was rescued by the Lord many times as I traveled alone, across the USA, Europe and in Central America.

What else? My dog, Lexie, sits at my feet as I write these stories. She keeps me sane, walks me three times a day and corrects my grammar.

That's about it! I hope you enjoy reading my Faith in Action Series and hanging out with Luke, Sara, Danny, Pedro, Jose, and their friends as much as I do.

46

Citations

All scripture taken from THE MESSAGE. Copyright © 1993, 1994, 1995, 1996, 2000, 2001, 2002. Used by permission of NavPress Publishing Group. Used by permission of Zondervan Bible Publishers.

1. Page 75, The Message; Nahum 1:7-10, 'God is good, a hiding place in tough times. He recognizes and welcomes anyone looking for help, no matter how desperate the trouble is.'

2. Page 112, The Message; Psalm 46:1-3, 'God is a safe place to hide, ready to help when we need Him.'

3. Page 146, The Message ; Job 8:22, 'Your enemies will be clothed in shame, and the tents of the wickcd will be no more.'

4. Page 149, The Message; Jeremiah 39:17, 'But I'll deliver you on that doomsday. You won't be handed over to those men whom you have good reason to fear. Yes, I'll certainly save you. You won't be killed. You'll walk out of there safe and sound because you trusted me. God's Decree.'

5. Page 156, The Message; Acts 18:10, 'No matter what happens, I'm with you and no one is going to be able to hurt you. You have no idea how many people I have on my side in this city.'

6. Page 161, The Message James 5:16, 'Confess your sins to each other, and pray for each other so that you can live together whole and healed.'

www.ingramcontent.com/pod-product-compliance
Lightning Source LLC
Chambersburg PA
CBHW061214210726

48294CB00006B/1841